Lucas

An Adventure of the Spirit

Jorge Schneider

Writers Club Press
San Jose · New York · Lincoln · Shanghai

Lucas
An Adventure of the Spirit

All Rights Reserved © 2000 by Jorge Schneider

No part of this book may be reproduced or transmitted in any form or by any means, graphic, electronic, or mechanical, including photocopying, recording, taping, or by any information storage retrieval system, without the permission in writing from the publisher.

Writers Club Press
an imprint of iUniverse.com, Inc.

For information address:
iUniverse.com, Inc.
5220 S 16th, Ste. 200
Lincoln, NE 68512
www.iuniverse.com

ISBN: 0-595-09696-4

Printed in the United States of America

To my wife, my mother, and sister who encouraged me to dream.

Acknowledgements

Thanks to my wife, Robin, and Keith Passow without their insights this book would have never been possible.

Edited by Robin Schneider

I

The wind-beaten, filth-covered boy stood thoughtfully at the foothill of the fearsome mountain. His squinted eyes were fixed on the enormous mass of land that at its peak seemed to puncture the sky. He wasn't just watching, oh, no, he was studying the shape of the giant with a hawk's eye. He read the face of the brownish-green slopes completely and in detail.

"Big," he murmured. Suddenly he shook his head; a growing discontent was striding forth. "No, it's not big, it's very...very big!"

He saw the sun working its way to the west, and as the golden star sailed across the sky the mountain shone even more.

"It's too big," he said again.

Of course it was too big; after all, Lucas was only ten years old, four feet seven inches or so tall and weighed only eighty-three pounds. He was a good looking boy with big green eyes, dark brown hair, olive skin, soft red lips, and a small nose, which at its end curled up like a clown's. The mountain, on the other hand, was at least eight thousand feet tall with a base almost a mile wide. This was no ordinary mountain, no sir, it was the very limit of the village, and its name was Fear Mountain. Nobody had ever ventured to climb it. Its slopes were filled with sharp razor-edged triangular rocks that could cut a hand in two in the blink of an eye. The grass was beautifully green but the ground beneath was very irregular, and in some parts loose gravel made the terrain very treacherous. As a matter of fact, there were horrifying stories about the danger sealed in this mountain. Tales that talked about little kids, like Lucas, who had disappeared one after another in the doomed slopes.

Lucas, however, wasn't thinking about those stories, for he was on a mission. Imperturbably still, he watched the peak of the mountain with the eye of a surgeon as the sun began sinking behind him.

Lucas was dressed in an old ragged T-shirt, which was very dirty and stained with grease—The same grease that is used on the railroads to lubricate locomotives. One could easily see at least ten holes in the smiley face on its front side. He wore black shorts two sizes too big. Actually, they were so big that his legs seemed to be just two needles hanging helplessly from his waist. The shorts had one back pocket in which he used to carry his old Boy Scout knife, a knife he treasured dearly, and a small flashlight. The zipper in the fly didn't work; however he didn't seem to mind. He was wearing filthy white socks and black sneakers that were covered by the brown dust of the trails. His shoes were loose, for they didn't have laces to keep them tight, so every time Lucas moved his feet he seemed to lose a shoe. But as soon as one of them touched the ground, his foot would land gracefully inside.

On his head his baseball cap hung sideways, Lucas loved baseball, with the inscription "Stars" right above the visor. The cap was red, white and blue.

Shadows were mixing with shades. It was the end of the day and Lucas was still scouting every slope, making gestures, approving and disapproving.

"Wow, it's really big," he said once more.

Suddenly he heard the sound of footsteps pacing towards him. He turned in a hurry to see who was coming. "Oh, great!" he exclaimed. Some kids from the upper section of the village were looming in the distance.

Lucas didn't like them very much. They were conceited and arrogant. But that wasn't all, they were especially unfriendly to railroad kids, and Lucas was one.

Finally, they arrived to where Lucas stood. "Hey, you, filthy little bastard!" one of the boys called.

Lucas ignored their call and turned to the right so that he could see the mountain once again. He remained silent.

"Hey, you coward, I'm talking to you!" said the boy who spoke before.

This time Lucas answered, "I'm no coward none! And say, you boys want somethin'?"

"Yeah! Are you still thinking about climbing that mountain?" asked the spokesman of the group.

Lucas stood tall and still and very calmly said, "Sure I am."

After hearing his response, the boys laughed and talked briefly among themselves. Then the spokesman of the group, who wore a red collared shirt, new tennis shorts and shiny white sneakers, said to Lucas, "Nobody has ever gone to the other side and you won't be the exception. You are so dirty and skinny that even the mountain lions will feel sorry for you before eating you. And the Ghost of the Black Reality…Damn! Man, you are an idiot! He's going to give you hell! Say, go back to the railroads and wait for the next rain so you can clean up a bit."

"You ain't got no right none to tell me what to do, no right none," Lucas said.

The kids laughed again. "You don't even know how to speak right. Didn't you go to school?"

"Yeah, I did go." He lied. He was a lonely and very poor orphan who had never known his parents. He had survived in the railways amid drunken men and railroad workers.

"You didn't go, liar. Hey boys, he's lying let's give him a lesson."

Lucas was terrified. He was very small compared to those boys, and to make things worse they were five! "Go away, let go o' me. I ain't done no wrong."

The boys didn't listen and kept walking towards him with enemy eyes. They were determined to give Lucas a lesson, a violent lesson.

In desperation Lucas ran towards the mountain, and went into one of the slopes. As he hid behind a pine tree he heard one of the boys say, "Leave him in the mountain. He'll never find his way back."

Like when he first heard the footsteps closing in on him, this time he heard them going away. Now he was alone and relieved that the boys had left. This feeling didn't last long, however. As soon as he looked around he felt thunderstruck. He was alone in Fear Mountain, not too far up, but a good three hundred yards at the very least. He felt terribly scared and began to sweat profusely. "I have to get out o' here," he said. He was thinking about the fears that inhabited this place, and of course about the Ghost of Black Reality. In a state of panic he went down the slope, and as he did he fell and hurt his right arm. In a condition of total madness he ran away yelling: "Leave me alone, you fears, you do no good to me none."

When he reached the foothill he looked back at the mountain, but this time he was crying. He sank his head in his shoulders and despair took over him as it had all his life. Slowly, Lucas began to walk towards the railroads on the other end of town. As he started to walk the mountain seemed to laugh just like the other boys. He felt, and was indeed, alone in the world.

Lucas strode the winding old trail keeping his head down and sipping his sadness. After hiking down about half of a mile he arrived at First Street, which was, as the name says, the first street of the village. It was a sad street, like everything else in town. The concrete was cracked and some rebel weeds were working their way out after years of confinement. In the center of the road stood a pale yellow line separating northbound from southbound. There were no cars cruising at the moment. The sidewalks on both sides were covered by old red tiles that time had turned into dirty pink. And lining one after another Lucas saw the old stores that once boomed with business now showing the empty faces of a bitter recession.

When he arrived at the intersection of First and Desolation, he made a left turn. His head was still buried in his shoulders. By now the sun had gone to sleep, and the night was finally free to unfold its wings over the village.

Ahead of him the town lay still. Lucas had to go through its heart to reach the railways, his home. "I hate this village," he said. "I hate it," he repeated.

Dishearten Village was a very run down town. Its people lived in eternal affliction. Quarrels were very common, and anger and frustration were present every day.

Lucas was an odd kid to the citizens of Dishearten for he never got involved in petty street fights. He also had sparkling eyes, which in contrast with the pale, hybrid of the locals made him a perfect target to unleash and dump the town's frustrations.

After walking three blocks he reached the darkest corner of town, Unknown and Desolation. He particularly didn't like this place. He had heard many stories about strange things that occurred here at night, and for the first time fate had placed him right in the very spot that he, very carefully, had avoided all his life. He hurried his steps and tightened his fists. He was alert and ready for anything; he was afraid, nonetheless.

Suddenly a shadow moved swiftly in front of Lucas, across the dark sidewalk and into the night. Lucas froze, only his eyes kept moving, scanning the whereabouts in search of the figure. He turned his head to the right and saw nothing and as he was working his way to the left the silhouette appeared with the quickness of lighting. He stepped back immediately and begged: "Please, don't hurt me none."

The silhouette stood in silence. This stranger was dressed in a black hooded shroud and a black cape that almost reached the ground. Slowly the hood was removed and a gentle, pleasant face came to surface. The face was that of an old but youthful man, with crooked wrinkles across his forehead. His eyes were as black as the night, and yet they shone like virgin diamonds. Right in between those glistening jewels lay a bumpy kind of nose, which made Lucas laugh. His lips were thin and pressed tightly against each other. "Ah…boy, I would never hurt you."

The tone of his voice relaxed Lucas, whose expression changed from utter horror to vivid curiosity. He scanned the figure and, feeling more comfortable, asked, "Who are you? And, say, what you doin' wanderin' the streets?"

The old man settled his eyes on Lucas in a tender and trusting way. Then he smiled and said, "Ah…boy, I would never hurt you."

Although Lucas had never met this man before, he felt at ease. He sort of liked the stranger. "Say, you have a name or you have none?"

"I did have one," the old man began saying, "but nobody asks my name anymore…oh, good Lord, I haven't talked to anyone in such a long time." His voice was soft and deep.

Lucas felt sorry for the elder, for he too knew isolation. "Well, I'm sorry you haven't talked to no person in a lon' time. If you want I can listen to what you gotta say."

The eyes of the old man shone with intensity, a shining so intense that it reminded Lucas of the brightness of the stars lying nightly on the peak of Fear Mountain. This sight startled Lucas, for he had never seen such brightness in any of the pale eyes of the villagers, and somehow he felt close to the elder. A closeness that no words can describe, a closeness that can only be felt, like the sweet heat and comfort of a warm bed on a cold winter night.

The nameless gentleman reached deeply into one of his pockets. "I guess I have a special gift for you, young fella, somewhere in these bloody trousers, but I can't find…Oh, wait a second, I'm such a silly goose, here it is." When his hand came out it was holding an old yellow piece of paper. So old this piece of paper was that one could barely read the words printed on it. He stretched his arm towards Lucas and said, "Come on, boy, take it."

Lucas hesitated for a second, then took it.

"Read it, come on, read it. Ah, boy, I wouldn't hurt you."

Lucas tried to read it. But he said shamefully, "I can't read none, I don't know how."

The man understood, and with a soothing smile said, "Oh, don't worry I'll read it for you. Just give it to me."

Lucas did as the old man said.

Slowly but clearly the man read: "Only in the land of dreams the marvelous flower of hope can bloom."

Lucas didn't understand. He had never heard about dreams and hope. He didn't know the meaning of these two new words. "But, what is hope? And say, what and where is the land of dreams?"

The old man laughed and said, "In time you'll find that out, I know."

Lucas asked, "Can I keep the little paper?"

"Sure." The old man gave it to him. "Now, promise me that one day you'll learn to read."

"But...I'm so poor, and the schools in this village don't accept no orphans none. I'll have to leave town to learn."

"Ah," the old man said. "Will that little task be big enough to stop you from learning?"

"But, to go...Where?"

The old man remained in silence and with serenity, that effortless easiness that comes only with time, pointed towards Fear Mountain. Then he made a little loop with his hand as though he were encouraging Lucas to climb the giant.

"Why, you mean that mountain? No man never climbed it. I couldn't climb no mountain." Lucas was terrified at the possibility of making that journey. He had always thought about carrying the adventure through. But it was just that, a thought.

"Lucas, read the paper, you'll do just fine, I know. I see it in your eyes." When he finished the sentence the stranger disappeared as swiftly as he had come, leaving Lucas all alone in the darkness.

Sharpening his eyes Lucas read his first line ever, of course he remembered what the paper said, but for him it was reading. He read it out loud, "Only in the land of dreams the marvelous flower of hope can bloom." He repeated it three times.

Hurrying his steps he walked past the old hardware store into the main square. This place served as the home to the most important buildings in Dishearten Village. The Governor's House, the Congress Capitol, the abandoned Cathedral and the main banks were there. All of them were painted black. As a matter of fact the official color of Dishearten was the ever-gloomy black. Even the flag was just a black piece of cloth as though it reflected the color of the souls that lived there.

In the center of the square there was an old tower with a clock on the top, of course the clock didn't work. Capping the useless machine was a wooden steeple. Lucas used to climb the tower, by clinging to the old stones of its facade, just to sit on top and be closer to his beloved stars.

Tonight he would climb it once again.

Placing the little paper the old man had given him in his left rear pocket, Lucas started climbing. One hand and then the other. One foot and then the other. And Lucas went on climbing, and like a spider he remained glued to the face of the wall, for he had to be extremely cautious with the tricky and slippery black stones.

When he reached the steeple he sat at its base and remained still for a while as though absent-minded; but he was not. Oh, no, he was now hypnotized by the splendor of the celestial bodies. Their virginity and radiance amid the dull blackness awed him. The stars had always proved to him that light could shine even in the midst of eternal darkness. Those tiny little dots shimmering in the distance were a feast for his forlorn soul.

After ten minutes or so of intimate communion with the stars, Lucas went into his left rear pocket in search of the note the old man had given him. He took it out and placed it in front of his eyes and under the ever-silvery lights he read it again: "Only in the land of dreams the marvelous flower of hope can bloom." He folded the paper and put it back in his pocket. Then he looked up at the night and sighed, for he felt at home. That sight filled his soul with joy and, for a second, he was happy.

It was getting very late so he climbed back down. Once on the ground sadness fell over him again, for he was far away from his diamonds. Dragging his feet, he began to walk towards the railroads.

When he arrived he saw the raw desolation that haunted the old railways. The useless signs, the parked cars with their little windows, all of them rickety, and the sad red and blue locomotives forever asleep.

Everything in Dishearten Village was in decay and the railroads were no exception. They had been closed twelve years ago, two years before Lucas' birth. He had never experienced the joy that a kid in America feels when he watches a train go by for the very first time. He had never ridden in one. For him the train was something that didn't move at all. Of course it was easy to see that in this village every aspect of life was upside down.

Lucas walked until reaching his sleeping spot, which was located right across the station next to an old cargo car.

His home wasn't a home at all. It consisted of three empty coffee sacks threaded into one big sheet, now used as a bed, and a little pillow made out of hay and newspapers all glued together in one little piece so he could rest his head. Two copper pans, which he hadn't used in a long time due to lack of food, lay on the ground next to an old tattered canteen that he had found near the almost dry well by the railroad tracks. This was his world. This was his life.

Lucas was about to lie down when he heard the very distinguished sound of a cricket. He looked for it all around his little world and found it in one of his pans. He was very tired and the sound of the insect was preventing him from getting a well deserved night of sleep, so he took it out of the pan and said, "Well, little frien' your life is endin' tonight."

He stood in front of the fragile creature, and bending his knee he raised his left foot. He was ready to crush it. The little cricket stayed still, with its funny antennas swaying from right to left and right again. It rubbed its legs making that wonderful sound that kids everywhere love. Its face was thin and well defined, and looking really closely one could see a pair of piercing black eyes, as though this lonely singer of the night had a soul. And if you have ever seen one of these little fellows, you know this is not a lie.

Slowly, Lucas put his left foot on the grass, knelt down and watched the cricket in silence. Suddenly their eyes met and Lucas was struck with a discovery so incredible that he fell backwards. After regaining his balance he kept looking at the cricket that, by now, was serenading the night. Lucas waited till it finished, and said, "You know little frien' you jus' changed my life. When I looked into your eyes...I saw myself!" And the cricket kept singing, but this time louder and Lucas joined in for it was the song of Life.

II

The morning settled lazily upon Dishearten as though the light felt out of place amid the ever-present blackness.

A tarnished sun hovered lazily over the village. It did play its part, that is true, but it did so with the apathy of an actor forced to perform in a scene irreversibly bound for failure.

The sky was blue, but it was a strange kind of blue. The elsewhere-majestic firmament was just a pale discolored imitation of what was intended to be. The thick air was mixed with smoke and smog. And due to the weakness of the sun fires had been set everywhere. But these fires, that supposedly were lit to bring some heat, were now polluting the environment. For these flames were fed with old tires, plastics, oil and kerosene. Of course, no one seemed to care.

Lucas opened his eyes amid the chaos that lay around him. He scratched his head and outstretched his arms and legs. He yawned not once but twice. Then he walked to the old public sink and tried to clean himself, which proved impossible considering the dirty old water he was bathing in.

When he finished he walked towards his belongings and whispered to himself, "This is it. Today or never."

As he got up and faced towards Fear Mountain, Lucas was invaded by a feeling that, although its origin was unknown, brought a state of anxiety to his soul. That good anxiety that serves as a prologue to adventures of vast epic consequences. He felt like a warrior, like a medieval knight in Camelot ready to go in search of his beloved princess. He carefully dressed for the magnificent task. He took the two old copper pans and passed a rope through the handle's holes. Then he tied the rope around his waist as though this old rope and pans were the belt and sword of Sir Lancelot. Next, he rolled up the three coffee sacks, his old bed, in one big roll, tied it with a piece of cable, and using a pair of old shoelaces made two little handles at both ends. Lucas passed his arms through them, so that his shoulders could support it. And flipping the big roll over his head, the now sleeping bag landed softly on his back. Lastly he clipped the green canteen to the rope around his waist.

Lucas checked his back pocket to make sure his Boy Scout knife and flashlight were there. He walked to an old black trashcan and looked for matches. He knew he would need them to make a fire at night once in the mountain. He found the matches near the bottom of the container and placed them in one of his front pockets.

Then, he went to the end of the old train station and walked to the only apple tree in that section. A rich man had donated it back when the village was a place full of dreams. He took seven red apples and put them in a nylon bag, which he fastened to the rope around his waist.

Lucas was ready.

Turning around he studied the railroads, his railroads, as though he didn't want to forget the place from which he had come. Lucas welled some tears. After all, this forgotten place had been his home for ten years. These old tracks saw him cry and laugh, sleep and wake up. Day in and day out the old railroads with its cars, locomotives, grease, signs and little black booths had been his world. Alone at night he had walked amid the cars and watched the stars on top of them. He didn't hate the railways. Oh, no, he simply knew that he had to go. The gentle push of Time had finally arrived, and with it an invisible force would take Lucas away from his misery.

Lucas was determined to leave. However, he was thankful to this sad, raw and forlorn land for giving him shelter throughout ten harsh years. He knew that the state of decay in Dishearten Village wasn't the fault of the land, but the fault of the impoverished souls that lived there.

Lucas knew too well that it is the people who make the land beautiful, for the land simply is. It is through human's deeds that a land can grow into a wonderful village.

Standing alone he promised, not to himself but to the land and this village—it's too easy to promise a special thing to ourselves, for if we neglect to do it no one can hold us accountable. "I won't forget you Dishearten, and I'll come back to watch my beloved stars."

It was time to go.

He started pacing the sad empty streets, looking in every possible direction as though trying to seize the town in his memory. He walked past Last Street, which was the final street of the town, but now, because of Lucas, it was the symbol of an epic adventure in the making. He kept walking across the main square and its buildings, and past the old tower with its clock and its steeple. Then he reached Unknown and First, and he thought of the unknown fears that he was yet to meet in the doomed mountain. Hurrying his steps he arrived at First and Desolation and stood still at the beginning of the dirt trail that no step had yet paced—bear in mind that no person had ever dared a journey into the slopes. He contemplated the terrifying land that, in front of his startled eyes, grew majestically tall until reaching the clouds.

He wondered if he should go back.

Gathering bravery from every tiny bone in his fragile body, Lucas began the journey.

He walked the dirt trail at a steady pace. His hands were around his waist and his baseball cap was still placed sideways on his head, as it had been all his life. To make the walk more pleasant, he whistled softly.

The trail stretched like a long thin noodle for about a mile and then turned suddenly to the left. By the shoulders of the trail there were many kinds of wild flowers. Needless to say, they were dry and almost dying. In the distance he could see the vegetation getting more exuberant but no more alive. Since the beginning of his journey he had noticed something extremely strange around him: the flowers, the trees, the grass and every single inhabitant of Fear Mountain seemed to reflect an eternal gloom. The trees were brown and green, that is true, but it seemed as though they lacked something inside. They had an emptiness hard to explain but easy to feel.

The first hour or so went by without any problems. It was nine in the morning and the sun was still climbing the other side of Fear Mountain leaving Lucas' side wrapped in shades and shadows. A light breeze blew from the south, and delicately played with his hair. At this point, that is, after three miles, the trail came to a sudden end. Now he had to find his own way.

This was a big problem, for Lucas was short and the trees around were tall and strong. He couldn't see anything beyond the end of the trail.

Lucas idled, sat at the very end of the trail, sipped some water and mulled the problem over for a couple of minutes. "Geeze, boy, I ain't got no luck, can't see nothin', now what?"

The boy with green eyes sank his head in his shoulders, closed his eyes and sighed. He was indeed disappointed. Here the trees were too big and their foliage overwhelming, and now the task of climbing Fear Mountain seemed out of reach. Lucas shrugged his shoulders and dejectedly shook his head. He felt defeated. But it was too soon to give up. He glanced at a tree and saw a squirrel climbing the trunk, and a branch that curved down in the direction of the ground. Suddenly he was stricken by an abrupt realization. "Climb this tree, that's all I have to do. Once on top I jus' look and see what's ahead."

So Lucas climbed. He grabbed the branch, the one that curved towards the ground, with his two hands and swung his lower body until reaching the top of it with his legs, which he pressed tightly against the branch. Then he embraced it pulling himself up until his chest touched the lower side of the brown limb. Once this was accomplished he rolled over it placing the branch under his body. Immediately, he stood up carefully keeping his balance and reached with both arms for the other branch. Anyone who has ever climbed a tree knows that the hardest part of the task is reaching that first branch. Then as you continue heading upwards you find that the middle part of the climbing is the easiest. Here the branches are close to each other and they're big and fat. But as you go up you reach the third part of the tree, here the limbs and the trunk grow thinner and they can break at any given time. And if the tree is very tall—this one measured about forty feet—the wind blows freely through the top, for there's not much resistance and the little brownish arms sway back and forth. Well, Lucas had to get to that third section of the tree and he was, as one can imagine, terrified. First of all he didn't know this tree very well, this was not his beloved steeple, and secondly the tree was at the mercy of the strong wind that blew on top.

When he reached the half section he frowned, sharpened his eyes and threw a glance around. He didn't see anything. The foliage was overwhelming. His fear had become a reality, he had to climb up to the top to be capable of seeing what lay ahead.

"Oh, my God, I can't climb no more. The branches are goin' to break and I'll kill myself," he cried.

Lucas sat there petrified, embracing the main trunk. He remained like this for two hours. Fear can stop you in a second but horror can paralyze you in just a fraction of one.

Lucas pondered the unwelcome problem. More than once he wanted to climb all the way down and just go back to his known railroads. He knew the only fear he had was that of the unknown, and that reaching the top meant confronting it.

Lucas didn't give up, nevertheless. In spite of his fear, he decided to go on.

So Lucas climbed once again.

Pressing his teeth firmly against each other he reached for the next branch and then the other. He was getting closer, but the branches kept growing thinner and thinner and the wind was now blowing fiercely, pounding the treetop with no mercy.

"Wind, go away, I haven't done nothin' to you." Lucas would exclaim more than once.

But the wind kept roaring and unleashing terribly strong gusts that hit the tree and Lucas too. At one moment the fury of the wind was so intense that Lucas was tossed in the air only to be deposited four branches below from where he started.

Lucas, after the shock, saw what had happened and cried for mercy. Then he realized that during the fall he had badly scratched the right side of his upper body; his ribs, chest, and shoulder were now bleeding and burning. He looked up at the top of the tree and said, "Don't be upset, I give up, don't kill me none."

After his plea Lucas began climbing down, and again despair took over him. Once on the ground, he noticed that the wind had died and everything was still. He glanced at the tree and shook his head. He had failed and he knew it. By some kind of miracle he had survived, yes, but now a feeling of worthlessness engulfed him.

Lucas had remained quiet for a while when a voice called, "Lucas!"

"Huh?"

"You've got to climb."

"I'm scared."

"I am too. But we are in this together. I need you and you need me. Please don't fail me."

Lucas dropped his eyes and sighed. He sort of recognized that voice, yet he couldn't pinpoint its origin. And for some reason he felt it would be a terrible mistake not to acknowledge it.

"I hope you know what you doin'," Lucas said. And he began to climb. Slowly, gaining one foot after another as his hands and feet worked their way along the trunk and the branches.

And Lucas climbed.

By the time he approached the critical third stage, his body was beaten and bruised, and yet he went on with the grandiosity of an army. Lucas, the conqueror, would not give up.

And Lucas climbed.

Suddenly and without warning, the wind howled in a ferocious way as if it were lost in desperation; but Lucas held on.

"I'm here to stay...you hear me!" he said.

And the wind answered with rage, but Lucas kept on climbing.

When he reached the first of the last six branches that stood between him and the top, the wind launched a new and vicious attack. Lucas could hear it howling frenetically in a state of madness. That same madness that an army shows when defeat is irreversible and trying to play one last card sends all its troops to the battlefield. But an army in desperation is not an army anymore, but a group of broken spirits fighting out of dejection, running everywhere and anywhere like an anthill. As the climbing went on, Lucas began understanding that real strength lies in the silence of the spirit and not in the howling of a desperate wind.

So Lucas climbed on.

When he grabbed the last branch the wind withdrew and suddenly the battlefield was calm. Lucas reached the top and yelled "I did it, I did it!"

Once he calmed down, joy filled his heart, and he smiled. Not one of those empty silly smiles that people carry around on their lips. No, not at all. He smiled silently; he smiled with his soul.

From the treetop, Lucas spotted the razor-edged white rocks that waited ahead. He knew he had to go through them, but instead of feeling terrified he smiled again. Lucas feared and respected them but he wasn't afraid anymore, for he had learned that the unknown, always so feared, once met becomes the known. Thus, this once unknown tree, was now Lucas' observatory, which he named "Big Steeple."

Feeling victorious, he decided to spend the night in the tree. He lay on a thick, sturdy branch and watched the eventide unfold its wings. And he smiled, for beyond the unknown lay the stars.

III

The dawn spread its blue wings over the slopes of the mountain. A new day was wheeling forward, and new adventures and challenges were waiting around the corner.

After having an apple for breakfast, Lucas was ready to resume the journey. He looked back at the tree and simply said, "Bye-bye Big Steeple, thanks for lettin' me spend the night."

He began walking knowing that somewhere ahead the razor-edged rocks were waiting.

The morning was clear and Lucas was happy about what he had accomplished the day before, and now a serene joy was lingering in his being.

Here the slope was very easy to hike. A gentle hay covered the terrain and the inclination wasn't very steep. There were hardly any rocks. Lucas, however, didn't like the silence around. It was just too quiet, like when one walks into a house and everything is in order. The bed is tended, the dishes washed, the newspaper placed in the magazine rack and the glasses stored away. The cream colored carpet with no stains and the clean towels in the bathroom with no signs of filth. There are no finger prints on the windows, no children arguing or laughing or playing, no stories buried inside the old walls whispering any secrets, no squeaking doors, no warmth and no living souls around.

Right at this point the slope seemed to be an abandoned movie set, with all its perfection, plastic beauty and emptiness.

Lucas murmured, "It's too perfect, too nice, I don't like it a bit." He knew that life wasn't perfect, so all this perfection around made him suspicious as though somewhere in this mountain a big conflagration was being orchestrated against him. He was experiencing the calm that precedes the storm. The silence of death when there should be the sound of the living.

The day was unusually hot and he had stopped several times to sip some water. Now his supply was evaporating, and that was a matter of consequence. Water wasn't just a fluid anymore; it was a priceless luxury. He knew that his life depended on it.

He was worried about the deadly silence and the lack of the crystal clear fluid.

He kept marching under the scorching heat. The trees that once covered the slopes had vanished, and only silence and hay were around. He stopped again and sipped more water. After drinking it he felt guilty, for soon his canteen would be empty.

"Don't drink no water you idiot," he said to himself more than once as he kept drinking anyway.

Although Lucas had been hiking for five hours, the sharp razor-edged white rocks were still nowhere in sight. He had seen them from the tree the day before, but he had climbed very high and the once almost at hand rocks were now hiding in the immensity of the mountain.

He idled one more time and finally emptied the canteen. "That does it, water can only go so far. I have to find a well," he said encouraging himself.

Suddenly he had an idea. "If I dig in the dirt maybe I'll get lucky and find a hidden well. I heard about secret waters that hide in the mountains." From his back pocket, he pulled out the old Boy Scout knife and began digging. What he found caught him off guard and astonished him, for under the bare hay there was only a thin layer of dirt and right beneath the sod there were rocks. Solid white rocks and no soil!

Neither secret springs nor hidden oases lay there.

He stood up and walked again. The heat was now brutal. He tried to moisten his lips with his tongue but he didn't have any saliva left. He looked for a tree so that he could sit in the shade and rest; he found silence and desolation instead.

Lucas thought about death and cried. He was too alive to die.

His little body was swaying back and forth and his once elegant walk had become a tentative shambling.

After hiking almost all day he finally saw the white stones looming in the distance. Once Lucas arrived at the very first rock, emptiness filled his thirsty soul. He was standing at the edge of what seemed to be a rocky desert. Here the rocks covered every inch of the ground and seemed to be part of a moon valley. They were sharp and triangular as he had once heard, and the brightness of the sun made them look like an army of swords ready to cut the flesh of the intruder.

Lucas knew there was no point in trying to go back. It was do or die.

In silence he studied the surroundings with a surgeon's eye and murmured to himself, "These rocks are coverin' everythin', and they go for about half a mile. To the right there's this big gray stone, solid and flat, impossible to climb 'cause there's no place to hold on from. And to the left there's a cliff. Oh, God! Now what?"

Lucas walked towards the cliff to see how high it was. Once at the edge, he threw a stone over and keened his ear to hear it reach the ground. He heard nothing. His face grew even more worried, for if one throws a stone from a cliff and doesn't hear a sound, one has the certainty that there's a long way down before finding solid ground, which in Lucas' mind meant a sure death!

Disappointed, Lucas sat in front of the rocks, under the burning sun. He took his cap off and tried to dry the sweat that welled from his forehead; of course he didn't succeed.

Lucas was stuck in the middle of nowhere.

His eyes were lost as though they were refusing to see the fact that, imperturbably, lay in front of them. He remained idle for a long time.

The sun began sinking as shades and shadows started to crawl over the slopes. Sunset was here and this meant, Lucas knew it too well, a descent in temperature. He had to set up camp and light a fire to stay warm throughout the night.

Tired and thirsty, Lucas rose and began pacing the surroundings in search of some hay, dried leaves and a few branches. After almost twenty minutes of laboring, he had gathered a fair amount of these elements. Without time to spare he lighted the fire. This blaze burning in the immensity of the wilderness was the only light in the blackness, which like a giant wing had fallen upon Lucas. This fire seemed to be a star yearning to reach its lost place in the night sky.

Lucas had set up camp on a slope and with him the presence of humankind was established. Mesmerized by the glow of the blaze, he focused on it. He saw the glistening of his eyes in the heart of the blaze, and this made him stronger.

Keeping his eyes on the glowing torch he said, "As long as my eyes can shine like you I know I can get to the other side."

Meanwhile, the temperature kept dropping and Lucas, due to lack of water, began shivering. He got closer to the fire in an attempt to get warmer, but it proved to no avail. It was going to be a long night.

The wind picked up and its gusts, as cold as ice, began to beat Lucas. He kept feeding the fire, however, for he was determined to survive this test.

Once the night tucked Lucas and the mountain in, strange sounds and howls began to roam amid the silence.

The blackness of the night engulfed Lucas, and he felt scared. Trying to avoid listening to the howls and sounds, he began babbling an old verse he had once heard:

"Stars full of Angels
Angels dancin' in Life
Life is a Star

full of dancin' Angels."

He was terrified, nonetheless.

Ultimately tiredness won and Lucas, cold and thirsty, fell asleep while repeating these words.

* * *

Morning broke and the sight startled Lucas: a fire, the very same fire that he had lighted the night before, was still burning. The little red, yellow and blue blaze in a heroic effort had made it through the hostile night. And as soon as Lucas laid eyes on it, the fire died as though its mission had been fulfilled. Witnessing this event, he smiled and said, "If this little fire survived, so will I."

He took one of the apples from the bag around his waist and ate it for breakfast. Water was still a problem and he, knowing this, tried to keep his mind busy with other affairs.

The affair of utmost importance now was to go through the rocks and reach the other side, and hopefully water would be waiting there.

He stood still in front of the white carpet of rocks and again he studied the terrain. After five or ten minutes he decided that the best thing to do would be to walk to the edge of the cliff and see what was there. With a steady pace he walked towards the precipice. Once at the edge he lay down, belly nestling into the soil, sticking his head over the precipice to study the wall below. He spotted some crevices and also an extremely narrow brink.

Quickly he pulled himself up and mulled the problem over. After a moment of intimate deliberation, of course filled with myriad doubts, he decided to climb down over the edge of the cliff and use the brink as a trail and the crevices as handles.

Slowly he slid his body down and reached the brink, where he stood still for a second. He knew that it would be a bad idea to glance down below; he did it anyway. Of course he became terrified. He wasn't standing on the brink of a cliff; on the contrary, he was standing on the brink of life itself! One bad step and he would find eternity a little too soon.

Tugging his lip he said, "Don't panic none Lucas, you have to be brave."

Surrounded by fear but guided by bravery, he began to walk. First he would look for a crevice in the face of the rock and once his hands were secure he would take one small step. First the right foot, then the left, the right again and so on. He did all this very carefully, for he knew that one slip could kill him.

Every muscle of his little body was at work. His mind was clear and determined, and his spirit was his invisible engine.

Lucas kept moving forward and never looked back—what for? He knew that he had launched himself in the quest of a new life. Happiness was waiting on the other side of the mountain, so there was no point in going back to Dishearten Village, for only unhappiness waited there.

Lucas went on, taking one step and then another. He had to be very careful for the top of the brink was covered with loose gravel. The danger of falling was very present and beating in Lucas' heart.

After a rough and strenuous walk along the brink of life, Lucas reached the end of the sea of rocks. He sighed, breathed with relief and rested his head on the cold wall of the rock, as though he were trying to ease his stressed mind. Once he relaxed completely, he outstretched his arms reaching for the edge of the cliff, and immediately climbed up.

Lucas had succeeded.

After walking on the outskirts of death for almost thirteen hours he had reached the lap of life.

Lucas sat quietly and remained thoughtful, as though he were giving thanks for being alive.

Not too long after he had reached the safety of the other side of the sharp razor-edged rocks, thirst struck him again. By now Lucas had almost gone a day and a half without any water, and this was a major concern. One cannot survive in the absence of this pure fluid. Mankind is not fully free, for all its glory and woes depend on the under-rated water. We are not that almighty after all, and Lucas was feeling that dependence in a brutal way. He was almost dehydrated, and his body was begging for a miracle to calm his thirst. And miracles, as you now, are very much in demand but very hard to get.

In a desperate attempt Lucas looked inside of the canteen hoping that a miracle would bring cool clear water into the empty and lifeless container. It is hard to believe that the presence of water can make a canteen so important. Whereas the absence of it makes a canteen a disposable object. Of course he found only emptiness inside the canteen, and this emptiness was one of epic proportions.

Lucas stared at the object that rested motionless in his hands and said, "This is really bad, it's not funny none."

Slowly the old canteen fell to the ground, as Lucas' hands began to rub against each other.

He was desperate.

IV

The green eyed boy raised his head and glanced around. He saw only hay and rocks. There was no point in staying there and he knew it. If death is out to get me at least it will have to find me, he thought.

In the midst of his despair Lucas was determined to go on. He had decided that he was not going to be the one walking towards Eternity. "All right boy, you are off," he ordered himself.

Gathering strength from his will he got up, but when he was ready to take the first step a question rose within his mind. "I'm off, but off to where?"

This was an issue of the utmost importance, for when one is off to no destination in particular one must confront each problem as it arises. One cannot anticipate or plan anything.

This very question brought about the sudden realization that if he didn't know where to go to find water he would find death! It's easy to run away from death when you know where life is. He didn't know, however. He only knew he had to go and that was it.

Lucas until this very moment had a goal, something to aim for. He had always kept it in sight, and although he didn't know what lay ahead, once he started walking he was sure of his final stop. And what is better he liked that end, for it was self-chosen. This time, however, Lucas knew that another possible ending could be a premature death, and this wasn't self-chosen. He realized that life, like a coin, had been tossed in the air, and on one side the face of tragedy was engraved. Death had placed her bet, and the only time the boy had to escape was the time that stood between the tossing and the falling of the coin.

"I'm off to find life," he said. And off he went.

He looked down the road and spotted what seemed to be a trail. He decided to follow it. Lucas paced the path until reaching a tall sturdy pine tree. There he halted, for the trail at this point diverged in two. This fact added more anxiety to an already overwhelmed Lucas, for he had to choose which one to take. Tired and bone-weary Lucas sat down and rested his back against the gentle trunk of the tree, closed his eyes and pondered his options. He tried to decide whether he should go left or right. To make things worse he was shivering brutally from the lack of water. He came up with some answers, but to every answer he found, there was a doubt too. Soon he got tangled up in the web of his mind. He was frustrated and weak. Still leaning against the tree, Lucas sank into affliction. He cried, but due to the lack of water, there were no tears.

Lucas had tasted his last drink of water almost two days ago, and now thirst was not a craving but a disease.

Disgusted with his mind he shut it down and emptied it of all its thoughts, reaching a state of calmness fully unknown to him. In this state of peace he waited for an answer. Slowly like the flow of the evening tide towards the coast a feeling made him lean towards the left. He ignored his intuition. But in a matter of seconds the feeling grew so intense that he had to listen. Something inside of him was pointing left.

He sighed and said, "Left, so be it."

He rose and took one little step and then another. His body was swaying back and forth, his hands were two dead soldiers hanging from his humanity, and his eyes were almost closed.

Here the trail was dark and the terrain rugged and treacherous. Lucas tripped more than once.

Again the thought of giving up folded him in, yet he kept going.

Lucas was a soldier on a mission, a pilot delivering the sacred mail from France to Argentina, a mother in search of her lost daughter, a noble doctor driving towards his patient whose very life depends upon his gracious hands.

He walked heroically all through the night. More than once his weakened body gave up and he fell flat on the hay of the indifferent mountain.

He had been with no water for two days and a half.

In this crusade Lucas understood that life goes on in spite of our sufferings, and that we can only share our joys and disappointments with our fellow humans; the elements are just elements. Here in the crest of his despair he began yearning for only one thing: human warmth. And this alone gave him the courage to go on, for he wanted to experience life with those souls that, like old friends in a night of vigil, were waiting across the mountain. Suddenly those strangers became his invisible army, his family, his country. Now he wanted to find water not just to spare his life, but to be able to walk amid those who were playing life in the village across death. Lucas, now more than ever, wanted to live so he could play out his role in existence.

Conquered by tiredness he fell to the ground, and as he was closing his eyes he noticed that the soil here was kind of humid, and that grass was replacing hay. This moisture was a good omen. He heard a soft vague rumbling. He keened his ear and heard the steady flow of water. Somewhere in the distance the priceless fluid was running.

Using every muscle in his body he followed the sweet sound. A miracle was around the bend. He walked straight for one fifth of a mile and then turned slightly to the right. Suddenly he saw it. Right in front of his bewildered eyes ran a creek, almost six feet wide. In its course flowed imperturbably the seed of life. The same seed that Lucas needed desperately. In the bottom of the stream stood some rocks that made the restless liquid take different detours, as though they were trying to stop some of the water for Lucas. When hope was nothing else than a fool's dream, Lucas had found life.

Overwhelmed by joy he knelt down at the edge of the brook, touched the precious treasure with his trembling hands and babbled, "To you I owe my life, my frien'. I never cared for you none, and always took you for granted. Please forgive me. Today I love you like never before. Today you are life. I won't forget you none."

Immediately after his statement, Lucas jumped in the wonderful oasis that fate had placed in his path and drank with long, long gulps. He also cried, but this time the tears of life welled up in his grateful eyes.

The coin had finally reached the ground and life had won. Fate had blinked an eye to Lucas. Whereas death had lost its bet. And all this had happened in only two days and a half. This search for the oasis of life had been a lifetime on its own. Destiny was opening its golden gates to Lucas' determination as though it were welcoming a beloved son. He had fought one more battle and in the end he emerged victorious.

Now, Lucas was closer to the fulfillment of his promise, the reaching of the village on the other side of the mountain. He knew, however, that he had yet to meet his biggest challenge: the Ghost of Black Reality. Somewhere in the slopes this terrifying being was hiding, and it was only a matter of time before he would spread his black wings over the cold nights of Fear Mountain. Knowing this Lucas said, "I know you are out there...I know." He tugged his lip and remained thoughtful for a couple of minutes.

But again, Lucas was overwhelmed by joy, for he had found the fountain of life, and so the thought of the Ghost quickly vanished away.

He filled his canteen and placed it next to him. Then, lying flat on his back he rested his left hand in the water; he didn't want to let go. Lucas turned his face towards the creek and said, "Tonight my friend I'm givin' you a new name, yes sir! Let's see...hmm...'Creek of Life,' yeah! I like it." Once this was done he fell asleep with the brook still caressing his hand.

V

At dawn the sun rose above the slopes painting myriad tints on the primeval landscape. Lucas opened his eyes, yawned, scratched his head and smiled at the sight of the stream. He ran both hands over his sleepy face, got up, walked towards the creek and submerged his face in the water. It was very cold water and woke him up instantly. Once this was done he sat facing the brook and ate an apple. Breakfast was taken care of, now it was time to go. A new day was unfolding in front of Lucas and he wanted to hike as many miles as he could before sundown.

So Lucas resumed his pilgrimage. It was a lovely day in the mountain, which now had a green face leaving behind the lifeless color of the hay.

The boy decided to walk by the stream, which seemed to extend all the way up to the mountaintop, just in case he needed water again.

Walking in a cheerful mood Lucas laughed at the capricious twists the creek took. He also noticed that here the mountain was beautifully covered with green slopes and multicolored wild flowers. This wasn't the frightening enemy of a day ago.

"Well, maybe this mountain is not that bad," he said; but immediately he retracted himself, "No Lucas this mountain is no good none."

The mountain was suspiciously tranquil today.

Was this the calmness that precedes the storm?

Calmness. Ah, yes calmness…stillness…serenity. Lucas couldn't be deceived by this temporary tranquillity, for he intrinsically knew that beneath the thin veil of quietude, the relentless fingers of virulence move at will.

It is strange but it seems that life moves like this: a sigh, then a sneeze. Before the most violent tempest there's silence, in the eye of the hurricane there's sunshine, before the earthquake there's calm.

These unchangeable facts have been haunting me throughout my life, and even today they confuse me: why does life change her face so capriciously? Why does something good have to be followed by something bad? Why does a hero need a villain to become heroic? Well, I guess we cannot appreciate our blessings if we don't suffer. Yet it is the suffering I don't like.

Lucas, too, had experienced this paradox. For a split second he was fooled by the gentle face of the slope, but that face could deceive him only for a moment, for he knew all too well that the coin of fate could flip over in less than a cent of a second. Knowing this he kept on walking, enjoying the superficial calm. His mind, however, was focused on that which cannot be seen but only felt. He was alert indeed.

By noon he made a stop to have some lunch, and to his surprise he stumbled upon a peach tree. He was delighted and stunned, for this was the first time that the mountain was giving something of its own to Lucas, the intruder.

He walked towards the tree, grabbed four peaches, and sat at the edge of the stream eating.

He idled for a second with his eyes fixed on the face of the peach, turned towards the spring and smiled; he knew he was rich. Amid all the despair and loneliness in his life he had found what richness really meant. Richness was to be alive! This discovery brought him immense joy. And now, by eating this fruit, he was giving the peach the gift of life, not a still one, but a life full of places to go, see, learn and enjoy. He understood the reason for the peach to ripen. It was time for this rounded fruit to leave the security of an idle life. It was time to move and leave the eternal dullness behind. This reminded Lucas about the nature of his journey; he, too, had ripened and had to leave his dull old town. He was grateful to the peach for its gallantry and kindness. This peach had come into being to satisfy Lucas' hunger. What good does a peach do if when ripe nobody picks it? What good could Lucas do in Dishearten Village if his soul having ripened had nobody with whom to share its journey? What's the point of living only for ourselves without touching the lives of others?

It's the interdependence of all living things that makes life worthwhile. The joy of sharing makes us grow. That simple act of giving, not money or wealth, but a simple smile brings indescribable joy to the one who's receiving it.

Astonished by all these facts, Lucas wanted to haste his walking so he could reach the promised town and finally share his life with others.

Today the mountain gave him a lesson; he learned it well. Even in the most odd places we can find kindness, and by that deed those places and their inhabitants show us their compassion.

Lucas glanced at the silent creek and realized that without the gift of water we cannot exist. Then, he stared at the peach tree and he understood that without food we couldn't be. We the almighty ones are so vulnerable!

He had found the source of wealth, which no money in the world could replace. We can buy trees, yes, but we cannot eat our dollars.

Here, in this quiet noon, Lucas reflected upon men and their greed, their countless toys and their never-ending struggle for power. He could not understand what the grown-ups are looking for. Why does everyone move in circles?

Hard as he tried he couldn't come up with an answer. He simply smiled, for he knew that men spend their lives with their eyes scanning the horizon, but missing the treasures that lie in front of their blind eyes!

Lucas rested his feet on the surface of the creek while eating the fruit and he was happy. He had nothing and yet he was overwhelmed by joy. He had fought for water and found it, and now the mountain was giving him a bonus. It was as though this formidable enemy were acknowledging Lucas' strength and as though Lucas were acknowledging the mountain's kindness.

Today Fear Mountain and Lucas had called a wordless cease-fire. Today they were finding each other. Today they were sharing life. And so, amid the sky, trees, water, and peaches, Lucas was rich. He had found the palace of a nomad, for we all carry this glowing temple within ourselves wherever we go.

Thus, we are wealthy simply because we are alive. Money, power, and fame are all useless, for without the miracle of breathing we would die. We honor money and power, and you know, here Lucas was honoring life itself.

Lucas and Fear Mountain weren't the best of friends, that is true, and yet both rose over their limitations to see the truth that lies beyond stupid differences.

Lucas had found and recognized a different side of the mountain. He saw the face of compassion, whereas the mountain acknowledged Lucas' bravery. They were still enemies, both playing their part: the mountain defending its reputation, Lucas defending his spirit of conqueror. But now they would never be strangers again. An invisible bond had been created between the two of them. An umbilical chord had been born to tie them together.

They were on opposite sides and yet they needed each other to play out their roles. The war had been launched days ago. Today, however, a truce had been called.

* * *

For an entire morning Peace was the special guest.

Lucas was delighted at the chance of spending a day without worries. He was free to explore the hidden treasures of the mountain.

This land had become a fairy tale, only for a day, yes, but a day can be a lifetime. A single day can give us a torrent of experiences so powerful that our lives are changed forever.

The joys, sorrows, surprises and disappointments concealed in twenty-four hours, can mold the character of a person more deeply than thirty years spent in a dull scholastic education. For living is experiencing and modern education is just the accumulation of knowledge. One, with no doubt, can respect science, but wisdom stirs admiration and reverence within people's minds. And it is not a lie to state that without wisdom the man of science would be adrift.

It seems to me that in our society we honor more the machine than the mind that brought it forth.

Lucas, however, didn't have time to think about education or wisdom, and yet he was receiving an education sprung from his primeval wisdom. He, the night before, had listened to his voice within and found the stream that calmed his thirst. And in doing so he learned that we must take ourselves seriously, for more than once the answers we are yearning for lie within ourselves.

As Lucas paced the face of the mountain, he also reflected on his journey. Now he wondered about his future. He had decided that once in the village he would go to school and learn to read and write properly. He was proud of his natural wisdom, which so far had been so kind to him. He knew, however, that wisdom without knowledge in the end is as futile as knowledge without wisdom. And that a real education should preserve our primeval wisdom while endowing the jewel of knowledge.

"One day I'll become a teacher. And I'm goin' to teach kids to read, write, and trust themselves," Lucas said.

Lucas didn't know what to call this tide of thoughts and yearnings that, like roses blooming under the sun, had invaded his being. Yet he knew something special had occurred. He felt stirred by an unknown feeling that brought him courage. Oh, if he could only understand that for the very first time in his life he had lifted his eyes over the cloudy sky to see the blue that lies above!

Around four in the afternoon he halted to have a snack.

While he was eating a little cricket came by and started singing. Lucas smiled at his new companion and remembered that other cricket, the one that serenaded the night back in Dishearten Village.

This time, unlike the first, he welcomed it and listened to the speech of the little fellow.

The sound bore no meaning for Lucas, but that which was hidden within was what he loved. He loved the sweet presence of life that the sounds carried into the world.

Lucas stared at the black creature and said, "You know from now on I won't complain none about sounds or noises, even if I can't sleep." He understood that where there's sound, there's also life.

"Silence is all right, but you know," he said, "even silence is sweeter when it carries the whistle of the wind, the humming of a bird, or the laughter of children." He knew that silence always finds a way to let life speak.

After the concert Lucas rose and began walking with a grin lingering on his lips. He had two more hours before sunset, and he wanted to cover as much ground as he could before setting up camp for the night.

Tomorrow he would attempt to reach the top of Fear Mountain. From then on the journey would be easier, for from the top of it, he would be able to see his glowing castle looming in the distance.

This had been a terrific day. Lucas had faced no hostilities at all, and now he had water and peaches to spare. Thus, like a shipwrecked sailor who in crest of his despair is saved by a dolphin, Lucas felt that the mountain had thrown him a lifeline, and he was grateful for it.

Around six thirty in the evening after marching the entire day, Lucas decided to set up camp for the night. He did so on the right bank of the stream.

At a snail's pace Lucas unfolded his old sleeping bag on the humid grass, and lay down in silence. He became pleasantly surprised when he noticed that right above his eyes there were no branches from the nearby trees. Thus, the magnificent night undressed its jewels in front of his gleaming eyes. The stars were shining with all their radiance, and Lucas felt again rich. Amid this majestic display of beauty he searched for the note, the one that the mysterious old man had given him. Lucas read it out loud, as though he wanted the stars to hear. "Only in the land of dreams the marvelous flower of hope can bloom."

All of the sudden, just as he finished the sentence, Lucas saw a shooting star exploding like millions of little fluorescent lights across the firmament. The stars had listened.

Startled he said, "I love you. Always." And this time a bigger shooting star made its way across the night sea. The stars had listened again.

Slowly, but immersed in a serene joy, Lucas closed his eyes and wandered away with the night.

* * *

Something incredible happened that very night. Lucas found himself as part of a dream. Not an ordinary dream but a stunning adventure.

Alone in the mountain he dreamed he was a battered, bone-weary, dejected soldier who amid the desolation and death of a battlefield, was trying to rescue the remaining members of his platoon, which had been reduced to rags after being ambushed by the relentless enemy.

Lucas could see body parts scattered upon the bloodstained fields. He could hear desperate howls and screams welling from mutilated bodies.

Amid roaring cannon balls and machine guns Lucas didn't hesitate, on the contrary, he launched himself in the help of his dying peers. He jumped over ditches, dodged bullets, stumbled upon corpses and fell over innocent blood.

One by one Lucas rescued those who were badly injured and in the deepest distress. Risking his own life he took them to safer grounds and encouraged them not to give up. Amid the pain and futility of a mad war Lucas brought forth the best of him and humankind. From within himself the unbreakable bond, the one that makes us risk our own life just to save the soul of an endangered life, sprung forward. That invisible force ever present in the heart of humanity blossomed inside Lucas, and with it the whole human race took a monumental step towards grandiosity.

When Lucas finished his quest he sat silently next to the shattered bodies to give them hope, sang some songs, and covered them with the sweetness of human warmth. Amid the cruel truth of a battlefield, Lucas unfolded his own heart with an unselfish love. He created a village of hope. He, who didn't know the meaning of the word "hope," was dreaming it!

And this magnificent succession of events was taking place in a night's odyssey, right where reality meets fiction. Does that division really exist? Chronologically: yes, out of the domain of time: no.

This dream was reminding Lucas that we, as individuals, are better when we cater to a goal higher than our own well being. For when we lock ourselves up within our self-built walls, our souls become poor.

When he awoke the next morning he was excited, but couldn't remember the dream in detail. Lucas knew that something had happened, and yet he couldn't express it.

He simply said, "I feel funny today...hmmm," and he began walking. He thought about that feeling but was unable to decipher its meaning. Knowing that everything unravels at its own time, Lucas decided to wait and trust life.

Today Lucas was hoping to reach the peak of Fear Mountain, and strangely he was still feeling uneasy about the fact he had yet to meet up with the Ghost of Black Reality. For some mysterious reason this infamous legend was being very evasive, as though he wanted Lucas to endure some more tests before confronting him.

Everyone knows that for some particular reason the hardest tests are those that we must confront at the end of a task, whichever that might be. Sometimes when we are close to victory destiny seems to toss in our confident way one last twist of events that most likely will make us slip, fall and lose sight of our destination. So many explorers have gotten lost right before entering their promised ruins, so many fighters have been slapped in the face by the invisible hand of fate when celebrating victory a bit too soon, so many dreams have been shattered when they seemed to be indestructible. And now, as Lucas was closer to accomplish his odyssey, he knew that an excess of confidence could bring the unwanted tide of disaster to his shore, and his dream could be wiped out in the blink of an eye. So he was alert. He knew that the Ghost of Black Reality would eventually show its claws. You cannot cross the ocean without hitting a storm, fly across continents without dancing with turbulence, or reach your dream without having to fight a frightening battle.

Every person who has reached the castle of dreams can convey that dreaming is not cheap. But not dreaming is even more expensive!

A life spent in the absence of dreams and hopes is an idle, futile, and dull existence. After all, the worst thing that can happen to somebody is to live in the web of nothingness. A life deprived of problems, defeats, and sufferings has no way of experiencing the joys, rewards, and victories that follow after those obstacles are overcome. A safe life is an empty life; a risky life is a full life. The rewards go hand in hand with the risks we take.

Lucas was risking his life, yes, but in the process he was living.

All the hurdles that he had leapt in this adventure: the tree climbing, the rocks, and the water had given Lucas the gift of molding a stronger character, will, and determination.

Lucas was now a better person.

He had become one with his soul. And who can underestimate the power of an individual who's guided by his soul? Lucas was now powerful, and maybe that was the reason that kept the Ghost of Black Reality away from him. After all a brave soldier may be a formidable adversary, but an unarmed child in touch with his soul is indestructible. For our soul is the very breath of life!

The day was clear and bright, with sunlight beams bathing the vegetation. The temperature was in the upper sixties, and there was no wind. Some birds were singing to any ear that wanted to listen, carrying the sweet sound of life through the mountain. Lucas was walking at a good pace, always with the stream next to him and his eyes fixed on the peak of the mountain, which now was getting closer and closer.

"Life, wait for me I'll be there soon," Lucas said more than once. He was very excited about making it to the promised village. His eyes were scanning his surroundings, trying to spot anything unusual. He found nothing. Everything was as it was supposed to be. The Ghost? Nowhere to be seen. Not even a trace.

"Well, maybe there's no Ghost," Lucas said to the wind. "Maybe it's just a legend. I know a lot of legends."

VI

Ah, yes, legends, legends, and legends…

How many times has the lingering coat of some unknown, remote fear remained buried in our minds preventing us from stepping forward?

And why are legends handed down from one generation to the next?

One might think, for instance, of tradition. But a tradition that shatters dreams and hopes is not the preservation of old cultures, on the contrary, it's a dead weight that is placed upon our shoulders to prevent us from reaching our glowing castle, our hidden treasure, our sacred garden!

A legend. Lucas was worried about a legend. About a tumor that, like some infectious virus, has been reproducing itself over the centuries, invading the souls of generations.

Legends are just that: legends. But if we truly believe in them, these tales of our imagination spring forward from our inner being, and become as real as the sea, stars and sands that paint the earth.

All of our fears dress up in some form of myth, so do our most precious dreams. But these black-covered tales, stories of darkness, punishment, terror and torture wrap us up in the thick veil of demons, ghosts and monsters. Unhooked from our sometimes-weak convictions, these inhabitants of gloom take us as hostages. They seclude us in a self-provoked hell. And their fingers…Oh! They are delicate as silk while caressing our innocent soul, but do not be deceived for these ogresses can devour lives with a voracious appetite. They're giant mouths biting relentlessly the purity of our dreams. Infectious poisoning bacteria conquering defenseless cells, fire burning forests, mad waters running out of control towards a little, delicate village.

These demons are the carriers of death. And Lucas was scared of one in particular. He at this time, although he didn't know it, was confronting the Ghost of Black Reality. For one confronts fear not when it arrives but when one starts thinking about it. It is not the task, whatever that may be, that we cannot overcome, oh, no, on the contrary, it's the fear that the task stirs in our fragile beings that defeats us!

How can one accomplish a goal if one is defeated already?

How can one dream about fairy tales and love if one is concealed within walls of frozen hope?

Lucas was close to finishing his task, that is true. However, that was a fact of distance. He was closer to the village, but his mind was as terrified of the Ghost of Black Reality as it had always been.

Moving forward, as in covering distance, doesn't mean that we are actually advancing. Sometimes we advance the most when we don't move. To move forward is to overcome the dark obstacles of our mind! Once this is achieved, distance is nothing else than a mere illusion.

Lucas was getting closer. Oh, no, not to the village, but to facing the greatest challenge of his short life that, like a hunter in the jungle, was waiting camouflaged amid the shadows of the mountain. Lucas could not escape his destiny. The battle, in his mind, had already begun. And it is precisely there were battles are first won.

It is the feeling of triumph, which, like a rising sun, warms our spirits and imbues us with the certainty that everything is possible. Without the magic of this silent reassurance we are already defeated. Souls adrift in an ocean of despair, hopelessness and affliction.

History is overfilled with armies that, like a death-row inmate, walk reluctantly to meet their tragic fate. Many a time throughout the centuries we have seen soldiers, already defeated, pacing towards the battlefield just because they have been told that, like actors in a movie, they must play their role; a losing role. And this calamity simply happens because some futile sentence has been reached and the platoon must comply with it. These men marching towards their macabre destiny are but empty seashells of the youthful, handsome, full of life men they once were. They have been despoiled of their own souls. Such is an army without the sacred fire of will burning within. It is this fire, the one that comforts each and every cell of a tired body, that delivers signs of hope amid platoons of despair, and like a soothing hand, caresses our cuts and bruises.

A war is a sickness too strong, too violent, too disgusting, which can only be overcome when we dare to believe in the power of life.

Lucas, like an army sent to the front-line, was marching towards war. He was about to be tested. He as a nomad walker, kept heading upwards towards his magic castle, which like a torch surrounded by darkness kept shining in his mind. He was so close, and yet so distant. His pearl was within reach, yet some unwanted twist of fate could take it away from him at any time. And destiny is full of tricks. Lucas could sense the imminence of war. He knew that somewhere in the mountain the Ghost of Black Reality was sharpening his claws, ready to destroy without remorse his bag of hopes and yearnings that, like a small army, was trying to conquer his domain.

Overcome by the silent tumult of tragedy, which, like a bacillus, was moving smoothly but relentlessly within his mind, Lucas kept moving upwards. He saw the sun heading towards the west, wheeling forward hurrying the end of the day. This very sun was a silent witness of a confrontation in the making. A reluctant witness. It was about to behold the roars, screams, tears and panic of war. Like an unwilling observer the sun tried to speed up the day, so it could leave this forced task to the bare moon. However, the golden star was caught between its duty and its will, and like the lonely watchman, who must keep eye on the fortress, its duty was to shine until the night finally unfolded its black wings. The daystar was obligated to stay, at least for a while. As a prisoner of the day it remained in silence, but present.

Lucas glanced at it and mumbled, "Don't go away none. You're my only frien' here."

This plea was easy to understand. For when we must walk alone in some foreign terrain, the beams of a golden sun deposit on our shoulders, gently as a caress of a mother, the warmth of life. Whereas when we are folded in the darkness of a foreign night, our spirits feel adrift and lost. Daylight, when alone, imbues us with hope; nightfall, instead, oppresses us with the loud riot of loneliness.

The day was wearing out slowly, but relentlessly, like water leaking through a broken vase. The sun was heading towards the exit door, ready to leave the stage. It wanted to be spared the pain of having to witness a confrontation. But, Alas! How much the sun meant for Lucas! How could Lucas tell the golden god that he needed it so? How could he make the indifferent fireball remain in the sky throughout the night?

The inevitable happened, and now the unwelcome shades were moving like giant hollow beings across the soundless slopes. The creatures of the night were finally awakening. They were not ready to roam their kingdom, for it wasn't nightfall yet. But they were becoming alive, however. Their first moans were crossing the land, as though they were sending a warning sign to a now worn down Lucas. The sun was hurrying its steps as if its contract had expired, and like some cheap vaudeville actor had to rush to the next small town. Ah, yes, the sun was due in China to perform at the break of dawn.

But Lucas, how could the sun forsake you? How could it turn its back on you, a child in need? Ah, yes, life moves in strange ways.

And don't we all? Don't we all pursue our duties and goals in spite of those who are in need, lonely and cold? What kind of society have we created, in which finishing a job in time is more important than assisting a child in need?

The sun was going away. No one likes compromising. How compromising becomes the act of compromising!

Lucas knew all this too well, for no one had ever stood by him. He was a rose tossed in a sea of thorns, a plane caught in the wings of a cyclone, a ship lost in the frozen waters of the North Pole. He was alone, all too alone. And now the sun was deserting him too. He was sentenced to be by himself in the night...all by himself with a legend of terror hiding in the dark.

In the midst of this maddening waiting, every second tortured an already exhausted patience, every minute concealed an unbearable anxiety, and every hour carried the heavy coat of an idle time.

Lucas wanted to meet the Ghost of Black Reality once and for all. But one cannot hurry what is not here...one cannot confront what is yet to come...one must wait...and wait alone...

Alone with one's fears, one must make sense of the waiting. But how does one make sense of an unwanted waiting?

To wait for that which we truly desire is already hard enough; but to wait for that which we don't desire is unbearable, unthinkable, and inhuman! To the fact that we must confront something that we deeply despise, we must add all the passions, dramas and thoughts that, like a sea during a tempest, are stirred in our hearts, biting our hope and confidence like poisonous snakes with a mad appetite. Thus, all these emotions undermine our spirits. Suddenly the waiting becomes more dangerous than the event we must face. Finally, when we confront the problem, this rotten cell is so drastically magnified that its heavy weight becomes overwhelming. It is precisely at that point that defeat is irreversible, and like a giant wave sweeps us out from the trail to our magic castle. Burying all our hopes, dreams, and goals under torrents of sudden despair, dejection and pain.

Thus, when finally subdued, we, the dreamers, are reduced to nothing else than breathing beings. Alive, yes, but forever lost, forever dreamless, forever useless!

Nighttime was finally here, with its heavy coat of gloom and silent stride. One star here, another there, yet all of them out of reach, out of the tangible domain. Too little to feel at ease, let alone feel loved, like when one rests in a bride's arms. The green of the surroundings had a thick murk of obscurity, and the nearby stream was but a weak sound coming from a dark ditch. In spite of the penumbra round and about a battalion of just one child kept marching on. Amid the soundless life of the Stygian darkness the footfalls of Lucas seemed to be the engine of a tank.

And yet, the tight hand of emptiness was suffocating him...

...And this Ghost who was showing no signs of life...and this heavy waiting...and this Cimmerian darkness...

Oh Lucas, you were the only living thing that night! And it was terrifying to be alive.

The hours lingered in the indifferent web of the night. Trapped seconds that couldn't reach minutes, let alone hours. Idle time becoming eternity. And who wants to be the hostage of an unwanted eternity?

Lucas, you were yearning for the sweetness of a new day, but that was so afar! You were wishing for a miracle, but sadly miracles have a timetable to follow.

Thus, amid the thick veil of haunting shadows you were a prisoner, a hostage, a spark of life amid the umbra of death. Lucas, how cruel all this was! You were aging! With every footstep you took you felt the agonies of life tracing deep furrows in your wakening soul. Each breath you took was imbued with the air of hopelessness. Your back was somewhat bent, and you were just a child! Yes, only a child, but life unfolds itself without any concern for schedules.

So many things had happened, yet so many were about to occur.

You were like a salmon swimming upstream towards its destination. But, Lucas, did you know that some of them die?

Life was tossing you one and a thousand times over insane obstacles, and yet you were stubborn enough to keep going...It would've been so easy to quit!

Tell me my friend, as I write down your story, what in the devil kept you going? Was it the adventure, the challenge, the need for change? What strange force was pulling you to your castle aglow, like a fish is pulled to the hook? What amazing discovery triggered this journey? After all you could've survived in Dishearten Village, couldn't you? So,

Lucas, was it a bet that someone had placed on you? Was it but an escape from the rowdy boys of the village? Were you running away from who you were? What was it Lucas? What kept you…

"My soul…it was my soul! I want to live not to survive!" Lucas cried.

Ah yes, Lucas, it was your spirit…ah yes, only the spirit can craft life…

VII

It was mid-afternoon when Lucas reached the plateau, which was very good news for his tired body. On a rock he sat quietly, trying to catch his breath. He was exhausted.

Reaching the peak of Fear Mountain now didn't seem so afar. Lucas knew that once on top, this epic journey would be easier, for it would be a descending trail till reaching his glowing castle.

As any climber who's resting in a shelter would do, Lucas relaxed completely, emptying his mind from the uprising tide of thoughts. An almost sacred serenity reigned here. I said almost sacred, for the fact that beneath the layer of tranquillity a tumult was striding forth. This undisturbed face of peace was about to be rocked by the violent hand of a riot, which, like the deep waters of the sea, was rising to create an upheaval on the surface.

Lucas, the conqueror, scanned the surroundings. The plateau was as green as a golf course. It's terrain evenly shaped and smooth like velvet. Some Impatiens loomed in the distance, jealously guarded by pine trees, as though they were remote treasures that could not be disturbed. The facade of the plateau seemed to indicate to Lucas that everything was in order. But that was just a face, and faces hide invisible emotions.

Lucas, however, trusted the portrait painted on that plateau. He wanted to believe. Giving in to the weariness that overcame him, Lucas closed his eyes to the world about him.

* * *

Suddenly from the depths of the mountain a very sharp howl interrupted Lucas' needed break. This sound had been very short, yet poignant enough to awake Lucas. Without time to spare, he opened his eyes and jumped into an upright position. He frowned and scrutinized the vicinity. Something in the mountain was becoming alive. And like the phoenix that rebirths itself from the ashes, it could not be stopped.

Lucas searched round and about the plateau, but it was of no avail; a mountain knows how to hide its perils.

"It must've been a nightmare," Lucas assured himself and closed his eyes.

No sooner than Lucas had fallen asleep, a second mad cry rattled the silent terrain. This sound was not coming from an animal…It seemed to be the creation of a human voice. A mad voice, but human nonetheless.

Rising like the fever of a sick child, fear conquered every cell of Lucas, who was now trembling out of control. This shaking was that of a man despoiled of his gallantry, who when confronted with the enemy is incapable of taking either one step back or one step forward. Of course this leftover of a man is slaughtered without offering any resistance, for he's dead before being murdered.

The boy with green eyes had to take a stand against the foreign anarchy that rose within himself. Thus, Lucas fought to regain authority upon his unmanageable body. He had to stop the revolution. He succeeded. However, the real problem was just imbuing Lucas, for once the body is controlled one must deal with the terrified mind that remains, which is nothing else than a succession of thoughts moving in disorder. Our brain cannot keep under vigilance the myriad labyrinths of thought that our minds carry, and like a jammed freeway, overload our fragile cells. Thus, questions pile up one on top of the other, and under this heavy pressure the normal process of question, thought, solution and response is utterly blocked. At this moment we cannot but paralyze our actions. Sadly we discover that an idle mind means no action, no action means no life, and no life opens the door to…

Lucas couldn't bear all these questions that, like hammers falling relentlessly over a naked wood, were destroying him: "What is this? Is the Ghost finally chasin' me? Why can I not see anythin'? Why is he frightenin' me?" So he opted for the best thing one can do when trapped in such an overwhelming situation: shut down the mind and trust one's instincts. Lucas keened his senses like a wolf before hunting. This time, however, he was being hunted.

Ten minutes went by before the apocalyptic cry was heard again. This sound was unbearable for the innocent ears of Lucas. He was a beginner at playing war. One can only confront the virulence of battle when one is familiar with this plague. But when new, one must pay the dues. And one pays them with fear, which is the currency of battle.

As any new comer would do, Lucas ran away searching for protection. He found it behind a rock. He made it his fortress. And from the security of his castle Lucas glanced in all directions. Yet he distinguished nothing; you cannot see a howl!

Lucas felt the wind picking up, and like a storm in the Sahara, the mare's tail began engulfing every inch of the terrain. An army of clouds was marching on, swallowing every square of blue in the defenseless sky. This convoy of silent mercenaries was deploying its black blanket of terror. By now the wind had become a cruel tyrant, spreading its anger over the trees, rocks, and of course Lucas.

Nighttime had taken over daytime.

The plateau, once a serenade of colors, was now a wrecked ship tossed amid invisible waves of wind. No crew was on board, except for that of a helpless child.

And Lucas clang to his rock like a Moor clings to his camel when alone in the desert. The relentless wind kept marching on carrying its indiscernible troops. This invisible platoon swept with its breath each and every inch of the terrain.

Lucas was severely mistreated by the mighty rage of the wind. He was as helpless as a butterfly tossed upon the outskirts of a storm.

"Please, no," Lucas cried. He was begging for mercy. But every time he asked for pity the cryptic howl grew even louder. The mad sky was now dumping all its contempt upon Lucas. Rain and hail fell without a break.

Lucas was a hero walking on the brink of martyrdom.

"Please let go o' me," Lucas yelled, but this time only loneliness heard him. And loneliness answers no one, on the contrary, it embraces you with suffocating arms that round your soul with the strength of an anaconda.

But even the opression of loneliness can be broken...

"Aaaaaawwoooooooo." The howl was now closing in on the child.

Hoping to be removed from this nightmare, Lucas closed his frightful eyes, pressed his teeth firmly against each other, and clang to the rock with desperation. As he waited for the bad dream to end a multitude of raindrops and hail tapped against his face, like a drummer beating on drums.

Lucas was abandoned in the heart of a dramatic storm. Of course the tempest is not dramatic by itself; for the word drama is associated with the world of humans. It is only when a cloudburst finds us alone that the drama begins. After all a storm can only be measured by the destruction it causes. A violent and unforgiving tornado is not dramatic if it doesn't touch any human lives...but when its path crosses a human path...ah, the drama begins! Thus, Lucas was in a dramatic situation.

All of a sudden Lucas spotted a tree. "Go to that tree, at least the hail won't hit you there," he said. He didn't think of lightning. His mind, due to the circumstances, couldn't weigh each and every problem. As he was ready to run towards the tree a ferocious lightning, followed by its fireball crashed against the silent trunk. In less than the blink of an eye the idle green friend was reduced to a lifeless piece of wood.

Having witnessed this event Lucas couldn't help but place his head between his knees and utter a soft whisper, "Stop...please, stop." Not long after he completed his plea four more strokes of lightning rocked the plateau. All of them followed by rabid howls.

Lucas wasn't alone.

Taking into accountability the inescapable fact that someone or something was out there, Lucas raised his head, scanned the landscape, and then shouted at the wind, "I know you are out there! Show me your face!"

Nobody answered.

Lucas gathered bravery from every cell of his being. Standing amid the rain and the hail he yelled: "I know you're out there. Come and get me!"

Again no word was spoken.

After a minute or so Lucas distinguished a silhouette looming in the distance. It was moving towards him. This presence had a human shape.

Lucas remained still, scrutinizing the figure. He tried to make contact. "Who are you?"

Very calmly the distant stranger, who wore a black hood and cape, opened his arms and howled. Immediately the storm halted as though the hand of God had been laid upon nature.

Stunned by such exhibition of power Lucas stepped-back and mumbled, "But…who…and…I mean…who are you?"

The form was now only twenty yards away from Lucas. This shadow, which seemed to have come forth from the underground, remained idle and didn't bother to answer the impertinent child.

Lucas was trembling out of control, like a convulsive body. His just found bravery had vanished without a trace. Again, he tried to establish some kind of contact. "I…am…Lucas," he said. "What…what…your name?"

Ignoring Lucas' request the black figure rose its right hand, and with his index finger pointed at Lucas. Finally the stranger spoke in a deep grave voice, "You, child, must go back to Dishearten Village!"

"But…why?" Confusion and terror wrapped Lucas.

"You, child, must return. You must obey!"

"Return? No, I...I can't go back." Lucas said.

In a mighty demonstration of authority the figure placed both arms down, and suddenly the tempest regained force, unleashing its remarkable rage upon Lucas. After ten seconds this personification of evil raised his arms once again, restoring a heavenly calmness to the plateau. Then he spoke, "You, child, must go back."

"No! I won't go back none,"

"Are you defying me, child?"

"Er..."

"Are you disobeying me?" His voice carried a grave timbre through the plateau. That same timbre in which the doomed tales of catastrophes are told.

"Er...no sir, I'm not," Lucas hurried to say. Then he pleaded, "jus' don't hurt me none. I jus' want to get to the other side."

"Ah, the other side!" The silhouette pointed sarcastically. "You don't belong there, child. Go back, now!"

Gripping his fears tightly Lucas managed to remain still and ask, "Please...Who are you? and say, why you tellin' me what to do?"

"Who am I? Don't you, child, know who I am?"

Lucas could now see the burning eyes of the stranger with all their madness and uncanny malignancy.

The answer was obvious. "You...you're the...the...Ghost..." Lucas stuttered.

"Ah, you know."

Lucas knelt down and pleaded to the mighty stranger, "Please...I...I...have to go to the other side. Please...let go o' me."

Despair engulfed an already beaten Lucas. He had overcome too many tests, and now when his dream was almost at hand, this terror arrived. People can only take so many setbacks before losing grip of themselves. Before collapsing. And now Lucas had to overcome another obstacle.

"You, child, must go back." The imperturbable figure repeated.

"Please…let go o' me." Lucas began to well tears of terror from his green eyes.

"Let you go…Why should I?"

When terror wraps us up with its invisible web, it's impossible to think clearly, let alone craft an intelligent answer. A fine equilibrium within Lucas had been broken. How could he articulate an intelligent answer? And of course his words were useless even before being spoken. "Because…because."

Too little to convince the enemy, who perceiving a disorder in Lucas' mind, intensified the pressure. "I command you to go back or else…"

"Or else…what?" Lucas asked the question knowing the answer was doomed.

"Or else I'll kill you!"

These words perforated Lucas' already weakened gallantry, like sunbeams perforating shadows. He had been taken prisoner by the mold of terror, which with a suffocating grip was petrifying him.

What to say? What to do? Until now, Lucas had been confronting a mountain, which was a difficult obstacle, that is true, but now he was confronting an almighty adversary, capable of creating storms! This Angel of Death could chase Lucas down the slopes. He was not like the mountain, an idle obstacle, which once left behind couldn't come back to haunt Lucas. On the contrary, he was a mobile soldier with unimaginable powers. This intimidating figure was the tyrant ruler of the highlands, and seemed to be the very Devil himself!

Lucas mumbled some words again, "Please…let go o' me." He knew that when at war words are useless, for when one is in the middle of a futile battle one must play one's part. Even if the part doesn't make any sense. A war has two different armies, and they must play their roles even if one of them knows its doomed fate long before being deployed on the battlefield. Even if its role means the massacre of the entire battalion. Losers are always needed to bring self-esteem to winners. One man's tragedy is another man's joy. Lucas was on the losing side of this malady. He was sentenced before acting. However, he had to play his role. So he accepted it, and remained still in front of the almighty figure.

"You, child, are beginning to annoy me! Go back now!"

Lucas ran his fingers through his hair, bit his lower lip, rubbed his sweaty hands, shook his head, and breathing deeply finally said, "No I'm not going back none."

The thought of going back was as hopeless as the one of going forward. Lucas was playing tug of war between what he wanted to do and the terror ahead. This time the black figure didn't answer, instead he raised his right arm pointing at the sky, and almost immediately the hand shifted to Lucas. The clouds twisted with fury and exploded into a frantic tempest of wind, rain, and hail. In less than the blink of an eye the body of the storm engulfed Lucas, like the tempestuous waters of an enraged sea envelop a condemned vessel. The size of the falling hail was that of a golf ball, and it was relentlessly battering the bare face of Lucas, who fell face down on the ground with his hands covering his head.

"Stop," Lucas begged.

"Go back now!" The Ghost ordered.

By now the sky was dumping all its violence over Lucas.

"Mercy...mercy."

"Mercy is death! Stay and you'll die!" The Ghost replied.

"But, why? Oh, please...I'm hurtin'!"

"Run stupid child! Run or I'll kill you!" When finished the Ghost laughed violently.

Unable to bear the pain and seized by the dizziness of defeat Lucas rose and ran away. He ran like a mad man, yelling and crying, without destination. When one is out of control, the domain of space and time becomes blurry and meaningless, therefore, one cannot recognize places, let alone remember them.

Lucas raced amid bushes, rocks, thorns and trees. His body, once clean and beautifully sculptured, was now bleeding and bearing painful scratches, bruises and lacerations. During this frantic race Lucas lost all his peaches and apples, and also the Boy Scout knife.

Noticing that the storm wasn't with him anymore Lucas halted. He had run too much. After catching his breath he glanced around trying to spot the Ghost of Black Reality; he wasn't there. He noticed that his heart was beating at a crazy speed. All of a sudden dizziness took over and he vomited. His face was pale and expressionless, and his hands shook constantly.

Oh, Lucas, you were the very portrait of horror!

Many a time he had imagined the encounter with the Ghost...but reality exceeds imagination! Lucas hadn't been prepared for this nightmare nor could he have anticipated it. His journey, his task, his life had reached a dead end. A life in Dishearten Village would mean an existence in a state of bereavement. Whereas if he decided to go forward with his quest he would certainly meet Azrael. So what to do? Where to go? Whom could he turn to for advice? Sadly he found the answer: nothing to do, nowhere to go, no one to turn to. Again, Lucas was utterly alone.

This first encounter had been but a prelude of an inescapable war.

VIII

Encircled by the paralyzing hand of terror, Lucas felt defeated.

This little boy with green eyes and gentle manners was but a body emptied of a soul, an ocean deprived of its tides, a tree denied the right to blossom. And a boy despoiled of his right to bloom becomes and idle elder, who in his desperation counts the seconds, minutes, hours, days, weeks, months and years that separate his heavy life from a weight-less death. The relief of Azrael is the only bearable future for his growing malady. Thus, the elder hastens the remaining time by shielding himself from the agonies and ecstasies of life. He becomes numb.

One must not go too far to find the shadows of these impoverished beings, which in their tragedy have sent their souls into exile. This state of being is but a frozen ocean that, like the perennial snow of the Andes, engulfs all those who in the midst of their quest have thrown in the towel. Once this is done life as we dream it ceases to be.

Lucas lay flat on the gentle green blanket staring at the sky. The storm had vanished, leaving just one or two drifting ships in the black belt of the heavens. Now, myriad silvery eyes were looking down at Lucas. These far and untouchable diamonds, suspended infinitely in the immensity of the dark vault of the night, were the sad witnesses of a tragedy in the making. Another Saint-Exupery was about to be put to the sword. This child, this rose, this jewel of creation would never craft his soul and reach the glory of his dreams. A saint was dwindling away.

High above the domain of the mundane, the remote gems glistened with mad intensity. Mad intensity, yes, but a sane one. Sane I say, for the simple fact that when the suffocating hand of despair grips a weary spirit, only the sacred delirium sprung forth from the abyss of the soul can save life. This extra-ordinary madness, please don't be confused, has nothing to do with that of wild emotions taking over the mind, on the contrary, this is a madness welled from the sudden realization of our right to be. And when one is convinced of this fact, one fights like a hero of beyond. For at that moment nothing weighs more heavily than our own will. And will builds. Will moves mountains, discovers oases buried in burning sands, and rises over the nothingness of white cotton-like clouds to see, with bewildered eyes, the grandeur of a clear sky!

Yes…to find life one must rise over death.

Those millions of silvery dots hovering in the night were giving Lucas a thread of hope. For even light can be found amid the darkness of the universe.

Oh, if Lucas could only understand!

* * *

An effort of epic proportions is required to escape from the sticky web of sadness and depression. The problem is that such an intrinsically complicated web has been threaded by our own mind! At this moment to follow the mind is to give up. Minds are strange and unpredictable, yet we must overcome them if we are to reach our soul.

"Why struggle?" Lucas' mind said. Then it continued: "After you, another poor soul would soon be gone…such is life! Dreamers are just dreamers…"

Of course every peasant in Dishearten Village would have an explanation for the failure of this lovely child. And all those already dead inhabitants would then go back to their daily duties, convinced that what rules people's lives is the reality around them. Ah, but these wise people are missing a rather important fact: it is us, when we have the courage to follow our dreams, who reinstate hope into society!

The stars, meanwhile, kept glistening, sending flashes of hope to a forlorn child. But Lucas couldn't be reached by anything. He was detached from his feelings, like a patient in a state of coma is detached from the outer world. He was but a hollow body drifting towards the void.

And how can anybody rescue a terminally ill patient? What kind of miracle could restore Lucas to life? What would it take?

Oh, Lucas, Life was welling tears for you!

The silent veil of affliction was now covering the child's face.

And what could save Lucas?

The stars tried again, this time dropping a tear. Immediately a diamond crossed the firmament. Then, another shooting tear took off. By now the stars were painting the blackness round and about with the tenderness of glistening tears welling from the heart of the galaxy.

Suddenly, Lucas was struck by a revelation, a sudden illumination, like that of a man of science when he finally solves the equation that was puzzling him.

"If I get up and walk, I'll be movin'. If I'm movin', I'm alive," the child said.

Through a sudden enlightenment, Lucas understood that what saves humankind is the willingness to move forward. The irrevocable determination to stride eagerly into the future!

Lucas was being reborn, still afraid, but willing to take a step and then another. And with each inch that he covered, a torrent of life began to circulate within his veins, arteries, bones, organs, and muscles. Life was embracing Lucas as though he were a prodigal son. Entwined with this blossom of energy he grew stronger. The platoon of just one child was again moving forward. And although Lucas had lost one battle, the war remained undecided.

* * *

Lucas, the conqueror, was forced to move forward and continue the strenuous march till reaching the outskirts of the Ghost's kingdom. New blood would be spattered upon the dark fields on which armies meet.

Again, this silent and endless pilgrimage, filled with the memories of a recent failure, took a toll on Lucas' bravery. His mind could barely withstand the myriad of thoughts that swayed back and forth within its domain.

To understand what Lucas felt one must comprehend what takes place when a troop is sent to the front-line.

When the war is new and still distant, and a battalion of simple men is about to leave port to embark upon a mission, which later will prove to be futile, one can feel in the air the exuberance of triumph covering the grounds, upon which civilians and soldiers embrace, wish luck, kiss and exchange hand-shakes. At this time, a thoughtless time, no power in the universe can undermine the confidence instilled in the troop's hearts. Unfortunately, the handsome and youthful army is intoxicated with some kind of cheap and lethal wine, which has been poisoned by the hand of a crooked future. And later on, when the platoon is alone in the middle of the journey, this venom will take row, and with macabre fingers will torture the souls of the lieutenants, sergeants, and soldiers who are due to the front. In a desperate attempt to soothe the rest, one of the soldiers shall rise to play a joke, which no one shall listen to, let alone laugh at. For in the middle of this doomed comedy, this army is already buried beneath infinite layers of speculations. No one real yet, but all of them moving relentlessly over their lives. And then, when finally at war, the soldiers will replace the friendly embraces, kisses and handshakes, for the evil of gunpowder, bullets and death. All these warriors will become heroes.

Ah, yes…but heroes die…and thus, all the affection that once nursed them will remain intact, but with no one to nurture!

Lucas' mind kept playing all these images, which of course followed no order. Order belongs to perspective. But when at risk there's no perspective, just immediate problems that need immediate responses. Future and past fade away, and so, only the present remains. And a life deprived of treasured memories and future hope loses identity. Thus, when this happens the individual ceases to be, leaving the detached soul with no reason to remain alive. For when all the ties that bond us to our loved ones have been cut to be dead or alive makes no difference at all.

Lucas wanted to be restored to life. He was yearning to see tender smiles and hear kind words. This boy wished to be in the middle of the human comedy with all its comings and goings. The cruel feeling of living a hollow life was as terrifying as the one instilled in him by the Ghost of Black Reality.

Before Lucas even noticed, he reached the plateau again. Every single inch of the terrain was wrapped in the sweet calmness of serenity. The rocks, the trees, the flowers, and even the grass, all of them witnesses of the first doomed battle, showed no emotion at the sight of Lucas. Ah, yes…rocks are inanimate objects. The fate of the first collision could only be traced in Lucas' mind. For the drama of life is to be found within ourselves, the players.

After weighing what the next step should be, Lucas decided to wait for the Ghost to come to him. When at war, to scout the enemy's moves gives us the upper hand. Knowing this fact, he hid behind the same rock that had sheltered him the first time around. Swiftly, Lucas lay down using the rock as his shield. Seconds, minutes and hours went by, with nothing important to take into account.

It was obvious that the Ghost wouldn't make the first move.

A psychological tug of war was being played.

One must point out that it is the challenger who must first step into the ring. Champions are reserved the honor of being the main attraction. Acknowledging this inescapable fact Lucas got up, and stood still in front of his rock, then he shouted, "Come on, you good for nothin' ugly cockroach. Where are you?"

Ah, but celebrities must be called several times onto stage.

"Oh, come on! You stupid Ghost. I'm jus' a child. Go ahead kill me! What is wron' with you?"

Ah, but celebrities are always late.

"If you don't come I'll claim this land as my own. Come on, you bastard!"

"Aaaaaawwoooooooo! This time I will kill you. You insolent child!"

Ah, yes…celebrities…when they finally arrive…they do so in style!

Swiftly, The Ghost shambled towards Lucas. This monster was lost in a desperate rage. Giant fireballs were being spitted from the depths of his eyes, which burned with the rotten seed of hatred. His hands waved frenetically in the air while his fists remained tightly closed.

Hey, Lucas, now what?

This time the boy with green eyes was determined to confront the evil being. Lucas remained still in front of the mad figure, and with piercing eyes said, "Show me your powers, come on!"

And tragedy struck.

In less than the blink of an eye, two perfectly symmetric fireballs came forth from the eyes of the beast. Lucas was hit on his arms, which instantly burned, spreading an unbearable pain upon his body. Lucas' skin had been lacerated. For the first time in his journey, this child had been severely wounded. Prisoner of pain, Lucas fell on the ground and began crying. Suddenly he rose and ran desperately. He ran without direction. But before disappearing he yelled, "You're hurtin' me! I'm goin' back!"

"Don't ever come back, you, stupid child! Don't you ever dare to come back!" And the Ghost laughed insanely.

* * *

Utterly out of breath, defeated by exhaustion one can only run so much, Lucas halted. Then he fell knee deep in the creek, the same stream that not so long ago had saved his life. Now the child's breathing was out of rhythm and lacked a consistent pattern, like an orchestra following the orders of a drunken conductor. Lucas' body was but a wreckage of the once handsome boy, and his face was pale and distorted.

When a tragedy is fresh, we cannot immediately react to the shock that rocked us. For we are but a living tumult. Later on, when we realize the magnitude of the catastrophe, and our own helplessness to twist a doomed fate, a period of mourning begins, and finally acceptance settles.

Contrary to what has many a time been portrayed in myriad films, when defeat is irreversible, anger melts away. Anger is a sign that victory is still possible. Thus, when the coin of fate has finally fallen upon the ground, showing the side of tails against our chosen heads, the play is over. And like an aftershock following an earthquake, actors accept their fate. This is a universal rule.

Lucas was now resigned to his doomed fate. He had tried to overcome the Ghost and the overwhelming odds against his quest, which now seemed to be merely a charade. He had lost. And it was all in a day's work.

Lucas had gone beyond the realm of emotions, for emotions are but weapons that one carries when in battle. At this point there were no more problems to weigh or decisions to make. The struggle was over. And following that fact a heavy cloud was lifted from Lucas' back. This boy was now spared the sorrows and joys of existence. Emotions were no longer needed.

Lucas had fought and lost. That was it. Nothing to add to this tragedy. No more adventures awaited him. No more campaigns to embark upon. And again, all had happened in a day's work.

Lucas had no more duties to carry through. After one quits, responsibility is a quality no longer needed.

But is quitting a natural action for us, the conquerors? And if it is, why is the human race so stubborn when it comes to move forward? Why do we strive so tenaciously to overcome ourselves?

If something in the human race strikes me, and it does so right to the bone, it is the willingness to sacrifice lives in order to attain a higher goal.

Quite often, while building a bridge to gap two isolated shores, many laborers die. And when this occurs the task is not stopped, on the contrary, the reaction that wells from the remaining crew is precisely the opposite. These men and women, after being hammered by the death of some co-workers, seem to be even more determined to finish that bridge than before, when they were at the dawn of the task. This fistful of laborious humble workers will stubbornly build the bridge in memory of the dead workmen. This crew unconsciously knows that men and women are but a tool serving to the advance of humankind. They, in their gesture, are acknowledging that by their effort and sacrifice an entire generation will move forward.

And how many times have we read, in total bewilderment, about a firefighter, who in the crest of a firestorm, steps without hesitation inside a burning building to save a stranger?

And last, more than once I have seen complete strangers, who when witnessing a tragedy, risk their own lives for the lives of others.

So, what higher force makes ordinary people willing to lose their own lives for all those who are in danger, as though it were a natural process of elimination? What weighs more heavily than the individual life?

To me there's but one possible answer: the lives of the whole, when at extreme danger, are more precious than that of the individual.

If by sacrificing our own life we help to build a better society, our deed is not in vain, on the contrary, our deed is a seed that falls upon rich soil.

But to give up just because we might die…ah, that makes the entire human race back up a giant step!

Lucas had given up, and with his decision, we, the conquerors, also moved backwards.

Another soul had been disposed, and before this irremediable fact, something within the boy wanted to cry. But how is one to cry if one has been deprived of feelings?

Tears can only be welled from emotions…

IX

The kid with green eyes, now hollow emeralds, sat quietly on the bank of the stream. No words were spoken from his mouth. After one steps outside of life, one has no more stories to tell.

Outside of the uncertainty of daily existence one is utterly safe…ah, yes, but safety is too expensive, isn't it?

Lucas was finally safe, and yet he felt infinitely empty…and emptiness is too heavy to bear…

…Only Lucas' soul could make a difference in this distorted picture…only the soul can fill the cavity of a depleted body.

Lucas remained motionless, floating over life, when a familiar voice called. "Hey! Anybody out there?"

"Er…"

"Is anybody listening?" The voice asked again.

"Er…yes, I'm listenin'," Lucas said. "But, who are you?"

"Your soul. Do you remember me?"

"My soul?" Lucas was stunned.

"Yes," the voice said. "What happened to you, Lucas?"

The defeated boy sighed, raised the right eyebrow, ran both hands over his puzzled face, and mumbled, "What you mean? Nothin', nothin' happened to me."

"Really? So, tell me, why do you feel so helpless? Why am I so empty of you, so alone?" The soul asked.

Lucas tried to find an answer, he couldn't. Good lies are a stock very hard to get when they are in demand. "I...I don't know. Don't worry, you'll be all right."

The soul didn't believe a word the child said. Lousy lies are easy to detect. "I'll be all right? Lucas you've quit. Nothing will be all right from now on. Don't lie to me. I've been with you since you were born."

"I didn' quit. I fought and I lost. That's it." Lucas began to well tears from his empty eyes. "Look, I'm sorry."

"Ah, Lucas, you didn't lose. You defeated yourself," the soul said.

Such words were too heavy to bear, and Lucas grew upset. He wasn't a quitter. In his mind he went to war and lost. There was nothing to blame on him. Exasperated by the remarks of the soul, Lucas rose from the ground, waved his clenched fists, and yelled, "That's not true. Take a look at my arms! See, they've been burned. Don't go round tellin' no lies. You don't have no right none to do that!"

"You have gotten a bit hurt. And so what?"

"What you mean and 'so what'?" Lucas was infuriated. "It hurts a lot, that is so what! I'm the one who got burned, I'm the one who cried!"

The soul rose within Lucas, like puffs of smoke rising through a chimney, and spoke gravely, with solemnity, "I see. For you to get beat up a bit is to lose. But, Lucas, there has to be more within yourself...Listen, when you decide to build the life you want, you must expect to trip, fall, and crash here and there. It's all part of the adventure you must live."

Lucas, by now, had sat down. He had cooled off substantially after erupting like a volcano, and this time he was more open to listen to that invisible self within, who so stubbornly refused to give up the right to pursue happiness.

"Lucas, you cannot and must not surrender!" The soul stated.

"I can't?" The little child was puzzled.

"No, you cannot."

"But...why not? It's so quiet here. I know I ain't got to face no more adventures, but it's so peaceful..."

"Lucas, you must go on. Do it for me. I want to live amid adventures and conquests. I want to go to the other side," the soul pleaded.

Lucas felt uneasy with the soul's demand. He knew that by quitting he had accepted the fact that he would never reach the golden village across the mountain. A minute ago that was a decision that he could've easily lived by, however, now it was different. An upheaval was stirring within himself, and it was led by his own soul. This revolt was hard to digest. It had to be taken care of immediately. "Look," Lucas began saying, "I really tried. Oh, God knows I did. But it's an impossible mission. Why don't you cool down and feel grateful that we are alive?"

"Alive? Do you call this state of emptiness being alive?"

"I'm breathin', can't you see?" Lucas was attempting to persuade a very determined soul.

"So what's your point?" the soul was relentless.

"Well, we are...alive." Lucas was running in a blind alley. Soon he wouldn't have any more answers to defend his decision. You cannot hold a position if you're not convinced about its legitimacy.

The soul stirred an already high tide within Lucas, creating a tidal wave of emotions, thoughts, and questions. "Tell me, Lucas, now that you are alive, what are you planning to do with the rest of your life?"

"I want to...I want to...grf...I jus' don't know." There were no more answers for Lucas.

The soul didn't hesitate and took the main role. "You don't know, and you never will."

At this point Lucas was standing at the edge of insanity. This revolution within himself was driving him towards the free fall of madness. "But, say, why you sayin' that I'll never know what to do with my life?"

"Because you have turned your back on life. You're refusing to finish your quest, for the simple reason that a stupid Ghost attacked you."

Lucas rose once more, kicked a rock, and tossed his baseball cap up in the air. Anger was coming forth from the depths of his being. Engulfed by the storm of fury Lucas shouted, "Yeah, stupid Ghost, huh! He almost killed me. You're now talkin' to me 'cause I saved you!"

"You haven't saved me!" The soul was upset too. "On the contrary, you're the one who's murdering me. It hurts too much. For God's sake, can't you see we are both hurting? We are both dying! Lucas, we are both part of the same being."

By now Lucas' anger had reached a peak, and the fury was slowly winding down. After one screams, kicks walls, and tosses bottles against the floor a strange calmness sets in. It is time to reflect upon the events that led us into such raw and virulent behavior. And without time to spare we must stride forward or else we'll remain forever trapped in the swamp of wasted energy. The first emotion that wells forth when one starts to recover from the blindness of virulence is a mixture of guilt and shame for one's thoughtless behavior.

"I'm...I'm really sorry," Lucas stuttered. "I didn' mean to destroy you none." His innocent face was covered with tears.

The soul felt pity for this fragile mind. "I know you didn't mean it, but I'm dying anyway. Lucas, you must meet your destiny. You must confront the Ghost. It is time."

Lucas knew that his soul was right. However, he remained frightful of a new confrontation. "But...but...he's goin' to kill me. I don't want to die none."

"Lucas, haven't you learned anything so far?"

"About what?"

"About life!" The soul exclaimed. "Do you remember the tree, the rocks, the search for water?"

"Er...yes."

"You overcame all of them. You fought and at the end you won."

"Yes," Lucas said, "but they weren' like the Ghost none. He wants to kill me."

The wise soul understood, by the last answer, that Lucas was terrified and haunted by his own fears more than by the Ghost. He was afraid of dying. "Lucas, you'll die one day anyway. But when that time comes you must be proud of the life you have lived. There's nothing to fear but yourself."

"But, I may die."

"So be it."

"But…"

"Lucas! What happened when you overcame the tree, the rocks and your thirst?" The soul asked.

"I found new friends."

"So, who knows, maybe you'll find another friend."

"The Ghost? I don't think so."

"Lucas, are you happy here?"

"Do I look happy?" Lucas couldn't lie this time.

"Don't you see it, Lucas? You must fight for your right to live your life. Die if necessary. Show the world that it is all right to chase happiness. Dare to live!"

"You sure that the Ghost could be our frien'?"

"Does it really matter? Friend or not the Ghost must be overcome if you want to be happy."

Lucas knew that his soul was right. In silence he pondered his options for a minute. Then the green-eyed boy rose and began walking. He was off to conquer his life.

"Lucas!" The soul called.

"Yes?"

"I love you. Always."

"I love you too. Just don't leave me alone with him none."

"I won't."

X

Lucas, like the lonely pilot who enters the colossus mouth of a doomed tempest, knew that this challenge could not be circumvented. This was his ultimate fate. This time nothing would prevent the confrontation from reaching an end. The final battle could not be postponed, and it was now waiting around the bend. No more run around. No more delays.

The Ghost would be there; Lucas would be there too.

One could almost smell the presence of the two titans, for the air in the mountain was impregnated with the fragrance of war, which with poignancy was covering each and every inch of the giant. Nothing could escape the final chapter of these two warriors.

And Lucas marched in solemn silence. When one knows that a battle of epic proportions waits ahead and cannot be dodged, one speaks no words, for words at this stage carry no meaning, as there's nothing to weigh or discuss. Silence is the official language of an overwhelming decisive battle. The soldiers of a platoon marching towards a final confrontation carry no words on their lips. They are aware of the magnificent task and, like worshipers in a cathedral, observe silence. They silently cry, silently laugh, silently pray, and silently remember their loved ones. The magnanimity of the occasion bears too much meaning to be expressed in petty words. For the spoken word has been created to share a round-table with friends, but never to disturb a soul that tries to find itself. That is a private matter. An intimate quest. It is here where one of the biggest paradoxes upon which I have stumbled lies: when one is confronted with the cold blade of death one finds the warm hand of life.

Like the farmer who goes back to his farm after a confinement in the city, like the sailor who smells the salted fragrance of the seas after being grounded for several months, and like the priest who sees the cathedral he had dreamt of for years stone over stone finally built, one finds oneself in that which one loves the most. And when death arrives one finds out that it is life that one loves the most. All the agonies and pains of daily existence suddenly seem very tiny and insignificant when compared to the joy of being. When our final hour comes and we must stand alone at the portal of death, each breath we take imbues us with the memories of a lifetime. And at that moment we rejoice in our existence. We find solace in the ones who love us, and we love our loved ones even more. No person when lying on the outskirts of death thinks about himself or herself. One is not selfish at the time of good bye, on the contrary, one thinks about the welfare of those who will be left behind after one is gone forever.

At the time of death the word humankind finds a new meaning within the soul, and the individual finally becomes part of the whole.

A soldier who must die becomes part of the universe; and the universe becomes part of him. The one becomes whole and the whole becomes one. The life of the individual can only have a meaning if it begins, matures, and ends in the whole, that is, in the human race. The isolated individual is useless, for his or her life doesn't touch the life of others.

Lucas, engulfed by the sacredness of his silence was communing with himself, and by this act he was reaching out to the world. Lucas was grateful for his life, grateful to the stranger who kindled his heart and set him free to find his destiny. He was also grateful to his soul for bearing his shortcomings, to the stars for giving him joy, and to the mountain for the water and peaches that once saved his life. Lucas, who had lived a life of dejection and despair, was acknowledging the only truth in our mundane existence: he who has not lost himself dwells in hope, and for he who has hope everything is possible.

XI

Pace the sunny slope for half a mile. Then across the stream that flows steadily downhill. Continue southwards. Follow the tall pine trees to the left, and then come back to the right, bordering the back belt of the trees, until reaching the left bank of the stream. Follow its winding course for about half a mile, and the plateau will unfold silently.

By now the boy with green eyes knew this routine by heart. He had done it before. However, Lucas played it again in his mind. An old trick to divert the attention of the mind from more important matters.

Lucas did exactly as he said in silent words, and after an hour of a tedious walk he found himself standing at the entrance of the arena. More than once he wondered if he should go back and forget this crazy dream; he kept going.

Breathing heavily and with his hands drenched in cold sweat, Lucas said, "Come on, Lucas, please, not now. Don't be afraid none." These were words spoken to reinforce his commitment to the task. "…you there?" Lucas asked his soul.

Silence…stillness…and more silence…

Lucas suddenly halted, pressed his lips against one another and frowned with concern. Then he asked dispassionately, "…you there?"

"Uh…yes, Lucas. I'm here," the soul said.

The child sighed with relief, and loosening up a bit he rubbed his cheeks and nose with his left hand, and then placed both hands in his pockets and sighed again. He was taking time for the remaining fear to melt away. Then, Lucas said, "Don't go round none playing jokes...You hear me?"

"Uh...yes, Lucas. I hear you. Don't worry. Are you okay?"

Lucas nodded and went on walking. He was ready to toss his fate up in the air and play his hand. He had gambled his life before, and he would gamble it again. It was all decided and there was nothing else to add.

Like an old friend casually outstretched on a couch, the plateau sprawled lazily in front of Lucas. And yet this time everything in the terrain seemed different, untouched and virgin, like a stage before opening night. Lucas saw the rock that once refuged him, but this time he didn't seek cover behind it. Very carefully with piercing eyes he scanned his surroundings, not once but twice. Lucas did this to position himself well in the event he should provoke, upset or even infuriate the Ghost.

In the distance various birds spread their wings and glided the primeval sky unaware of the tension below. Some daisies were swaying back and forth at the rhythm of the light breeze that blew southwards. Amid them, two multicolored butterflies were making love to the plateau.

Nothing in the mountain could anticipate the upcoming duel. Even though the main characters were ready to meet their destiny.

Lucas sat on the uncombed and docile grass, and fixed his eyes on what lay in front of him. He could see the greenery gently rolling up and down as if moving in little waves. Scattered upon the turf some beetles crawled with no direction, and to the right a legion of ants were building highways to carry their stock. Opposite to Lucas a belt of pine trees sealed the north flank of the plateau. As a matter of fact, the Ghost had come from inside that tide of trees.

And Lucas waited. Now and again he tested his soul, just to feel secure. "...you there?"

"Yes..."

After each reassurance he felt protected as though the celestial wing of an angel had folded him in, and like the rugged terrain of a mountaintop capped by the gentle snow, Lucas felt covered by the soft hand of a beloved friend. He felt armored. He was now Sir Lucas, knight of the mountain. He was warm inside. For his fire within had ignited the wood, which was now cracking and sending forth fluorescent sparks of love. Lucas was at home. And home was within himself. No longer would Lucas be homeless, for he had found shelter in his soul. Acknowledging this truth, he smiled joyfully amid the serenity of the slope.

Ah, yes, serenity…so sweet yet so easy to break, and Lucas' mind knowing this fact suddenly interfered and reminded him of his unsolved duel. The human brain doesn't understand emotions or feelings. It just analyzes them with pure cold logic. And now logic was saying that it was time to worry about the Ghost. Thus, Lucas obeyed. He began drumming his fingers against his lap and tugging his lower lip. Lucas was indeed concerned.

Minutes went by…then hours, which fell like dead leaves of an autumn morning.

And Lucas waited…lingered…and waited…until…

"Aaawooooo, Aaawooooo."

Lucas jumped right up, tightened his teeth, clenched his fists, and touched base with his soul. "…you there?"

Silence.

"Not now! You there?" Lucas cried.

"Uh…yes."

Souls are supposed to be ready at all times. "…you all right?"

Silence.

"Hey!"

"Uh…fine, Lucas, fine."

"Why didn't you answer?" The boy asked.

"I did, you just didn't listen. If we both talk at the same…"

Suddenly the Ghost stepped into view. "You! You again. This time I'll kill you!" The Ghost erupted the words with rage.

"Wait!" Lucas pleaded.

But the Ghost ignored the desperate request, and launched war over Lucas. In a sudden act and without removing the black hood from his face the Ghost swept Lucas up with his deformed hands, lifted him high in the air, and tossed him against the trunk of a tree. After hitting violently against it Lucas fell on the ground. He was giddy and immersed in pain. He tried to get up but it was of no avail. Noticing this the relentless Ghost stood next to the boy and laughed frenetically. He spitted two balls of fire from his blazing eyes, and Lucas was burned on his arms once more. The boy with green eyes was being murdered. Slowly but surely.

"And now it's good bye forever," the Ghost said.

"Wait, please, wait!"

Suddenly a voice rose within Lucas. "Love, Lucas, try love," the whisper said.

"What?"

"Shh! Don't talk. If we both talk at the same time we can't hear one another," the soul said.

"Love?" Asked an incredulous Lucas.

"Trust me."

Meanwhile, the Ghost had taken a big rounded gray rock and lifted it over his head. He backed up one full step as though he wanted to find a better angle from which to enjoy the tragedy. A different perspective, a different sight. "Lucas your final hour has come. Die, child, die!" The Ghost said.

In a sudden move executed at the speed of light, Lucas turned face up and his eyes met the eyes of the Ghost, who for the first time hesitated. Lucas held a long stare and said, "I forgive you."

"What?"

"I forgive you. And I love you," Lucas said.

"You what?"

"I love you," Lucas repeated.

All of a sudden the eyes of the Ghost lost their mad blaze and demonic rage, and for the first time he looked extremely puzzled, as though Lucas had reached a hidden well buried beneath layers of blank emotions.

"You can't love me. You must fear me!" The Ghost said.

Lucas, perceiving a crack on the door quickly placed a foot in. "You know I'm not afraid of you none. I forgive you...I love you. So, if you want to kill me jus' go ahead. But I won't be scared none."

The Ghost raised his eyebrows in a gesture of surprise. "No,no, you don't understand. You must cry and beg. I am the Ghost of Black Reality, you must fear me."

"I know," Lucas said.

"Well...but you are loving me instead. Why?"

Life changes in a blink of an eye. And now Lucas had the upper hand. "I love you 'cause you remind me of myself, of my own fears."

"I am your worst fears!"

"Well," Lucas said, "I have only one wish before I die: I want to see your face."

"My face? No! Besides, now I can't kill you," said the Ghost leaving no trace of ire in his words.

Lucas smiled and said, "You can't?"

"No, I can't."

"But, say, jus' a second ago you were about to kill me, and now..."

"Oh, no, I wouldn't kill you. I was just bragging. My job is to scare you, but that's it. If I killed you I'd be jobless, for I wouldn't have anyone to frighten anymore. I need you to be afraid, but now..."

Lucas opened his eyes widely, shook his head and said, "You mean, uhh...that all this time I was afraid of nothin'?"

"If you want to put it that way...yes." The Ghost said.

"But, you hurt me!"

The Ghost drew a smirk upon his dark face. "I beat you up a bit here and there, you know. But that's about it. It works all the time. People get easily scared and they give up. They simply quit...but now..."

"But now what?" Lucas asked.

"Well, now I'm unemployed," said the Ghost blushing. This was a different person compared to the ruthless enemy of just minutes ago.

"Unemployed...Why?"

"Lucas, you have conquered your fears." The Ghost paused, sighed and went on with his explanation, "Besides, you just told me that you love me. And I know you are sincere. Lucas, love conquers all."

Lucas, moved by the sincerity of the words spoken by the Ghost said, "Let me see your face."

"No, please...no."

"Just once. Come on."

"Please, go. Just go."

But Lucas didn't listen to the Ghost's request. Thus he reached up with his left hand and grabbed the hood that covered the Ghost's face, and with a sudden move Lucas pulled it down, leaving the face of the Ghost uncovered. What he saw was beyond his imagination.

"But, but, you are..." Lucas was stunned.

The Ghost nodded, and remained in silence.

"I don't understand."

"It's not that hard," the Ghost said. Then he explained, "See, people cast their fears away. They don't want to confront them, for they represent a side of them that they don't like. As a matter of fact they despise those ugly demons, they reject them, and so their fears become their enemies."

"You ain't my enemy none," Lucas hurried to say.

"I was, Lucas, I was. But now...you have tamed me. You must go now Lucas. Just go."

"Er...I can't go none."

"Why not?" The Ghost asked.

"Well, I can't leave you here none. You'd be jobless. And I have an idea..." Lucas' eyes shone with intensity when he thought about his plan.

"An idea?"

"Say, I need someone to scare those who try to push me around and hurt me, you know…Want the job?"

"Me? To protect you? I am your worst fears. I was your enemy," said a puzzled Ghost.

Lucas shrugged and said, "Be my frien'. Help me live a life I can be proud of."

"Are you inviting me home?"

Lucas smiled broadly and spread his arms. Suddenly both gladiators embraced, and the two became one; and Lucas was finally one indivisible being. After the hug was consummated, Lucas found himself holding the vacant shroud, which had been dressing the Ghost. He dropped it on the humid grass. Suddenly a miracle took place: the black shroud, as soon as it touched the turf, bloomed into a rose as mesmerizing as a woman of exceeding beauty. Lucas contemplated the red rose awhile as though he wanted to store it in his memory forever. Then the boy smiled and began striding towards the village, which now was certainly within reach.

The war was finally over. The Ghost had found home and Lucas had gained a mighty ally.

As Lucas was pacing the plateau a voice called, "Lucas!"

"Yes?"

"Thanks…"

"Oh, you're welcome soul," the green eyed boy said.

"No, Lucas, I'm the Ghost."

"Oh…"

"Thanks for recovering my brother."

"Your brother?" Lucas asked.

"Lucas, you must face your other side if you are to be one. You can't live a good life without taming your demons," the voice said.

"Thanks, Ghost."

"No, Lucas, that was me, your good old soul."

Lucas halted, took both hands to his face and said, "You guys er gonna drive me crazy!" And he laughed loudly, for he was covered with a maddening joy.

XII

On top of the gentle hill, the boy with green eyes stood in silence, and like an archeologist on the verge of opening the sealed entrance of an ancient tomb, Lucas was astonished by the dimension of his own discovery.

Thus, the first sight of his jewel mesmerized Lucas, the discoverer. And like the captain of a long, almost never-ending voyage across the seas at the moment of spotting his promised land, with its tints of greens and browns, through some cracks on the lingering fog of the bay, Lucas felt tossed amid the turbulent waves of a sudden and maddening happiness. The green-eyed boy rubbed his startled face with trembling hands, as though he couldn't believe what lay in front of him. The view was indeed overwhelming. The untouchable was finally touchable. The firstly thought unattainable quest was now perfectly attainable. And now like in the final chapter of a fairy tale, down below from where he stood and towards the west, the magical hamlet unfolded lazily under the sunbeams. Lucas had made it. He had become a conqueror.

Acknowledging the magnanimity of the occasion Lucas tried to seize in his pupils the sight of the town, but tears of relief, joy and delirium kept welling from his innocent eyes. He ran his hands over his face to dry the tears, but it was of no avail, for there were too many.

Slowly he sat down and remained thoughtful, as he tried to put the puzzle of his ordeal finally together. In no time he realized that his journey was too recent to spring forth any memories. Of course Lucas experienced some flashbacks, but he couldn't articulate them. His recent past was in disarray as though the adventure had left an open wound that needed healing. Later on, Time would slowly cure the lacerations of the journey, for Time comforts all our wounds. And finally a scar would seal the open flesh, leaving a furrow in Lucas' soul forever, for Time soothes, yes, but Memory remembers. And it is precisely there, in the afterthought, where the lesson lies.

Under easy sail, Lucas fixed his eyes on the glowing village that sprawled over the valley. He sighed and thanked the heavens, like an explorer at the time of his rescue after being lost in the desert for several days. Once the cold shock of victory was absorbed, Lucas began to scout the hamlet in detail.

Lucas saw the stream, the same one that had helped him before, maintaining its course downhill while capriciously twisting from right to left and right again. Just before entering the town the stream widened considerably, at least a good thirty feet, and then it went through the heart of the village. Actually the stream was now a river, dividing the town in two sections. From the hill whereupon Lucas stood, the river was silvery, for the sun was spreading its gift of light over the surface of the water.

Uniting both banks, some bridges outstretched over the river. Lucas counted them; there were four in total. All of them painted in different colors: lavender, light blue, white, and red. Two out of the four bridges were for pedestrians only, and they were placed in between the other two, which were used to move the traffic of cars from one bank to the other.

The pedestrian bridges were hanging bridges, made out of wood with sturdy sailor's rope for handles. One was red, the other white. They were both narrow, and their belly seemed to caress the river below them.

The bridges transporting cars were designed in the form of an arch, with rounded white marble-like columns raising them high above the surface of the water. One was light blue, the other lavender. Both bridges were ornamented with an assortment of colored flowers, giving off the impression of being hanging arboretums.

The hamlet could easily be divided in two. The right side, that is the right side from Lucas' view, was spectacular. Here the bank of the river was wide and almost flat. It looked like a beach, considering its sandy formation. The sand was white as sugar and thin as powder. This obviously was the place to be during the hot and dry summer months. This long noodle of sand was well kept and clean, but it also had been endowed with the miracle of human warmth, for one could trace a series of footsteps that had been printed in its sugar-like face by who knows what soul. There were also traces of dogs and birds. And again it was clean, yes, but bearing the lovely disorder of life.

Moving away from the water towards the street, one could see the sand yielding, giving the right of way to a magnificent garden. This garden followed the course of the river and it widened at least one hundred feet until reaching the first street of town. On its closest side to the sand, the grass was dressed in tints of dark and light greens, giving the illusion of shallowness and deepness. The turf was humid, but not wet and the soil seemed to be very rich. Moving upwards from the sand and towards the street, the gardens presented a dramatic change. Here a myriad of flowers and plants were blooming in a waterfall of colors and forms. There were pink Lotus, red Field Poppies, Sweet Violets, and yellow Carnations.

This concert of colors outstretched all the way from the edge of the sand to First Street, and it finally ended by a belt of tall sturdy palm trees, which at their feet were crowned with beautiful red Carnations.

This side of town was the residential section. It was designed with simplicity, and yet it was remarkably beautiful. The houses were wonderful alpine chalets, perfectly lined up one after another, with multicolored lawns bordered by picket fences.

All the streets followed a straight pattern, dividing the town in perfectly symmetric squares. The roads themselves were enchanting, for they were made out of seashells, which under the golden beams of the sun showed their radiance. All the seashells were brought to town using a very efficient railroad system, which stretched like giant snakes across the valley till reaching the north shoreline, at least five hundred miles away.

The old railroad had been designed and built by the pioneers of Dream Village, a very special breed of people, who thought that failure was the stairway that led to success. They had been very strong-minded people, and had borne an iron will.

There was one peculiarity about the way in which the rail tracks were designed: they didn't go through town, on the contrary the entire railroad system circumvented the hamlet, and had stations on both ends of the village. They were satellite stations. Then it unfolded beyond the boundaries of town until reaching the end of the land. The reason for this special layout was that the citizens of this gem really liked serenity.

Lucas kept observing the town in silence from a distance. Suddenly his attention shifted towards the left. He was immediately struck by the architectural style of this side.

By the edge of the river there was a promenade, dressed with gray granite-like cobblestones, and at both sides of the street there were a myriad of sidewalk cafes, restaurants, shops, galleries, and ice-cream parlors.

Lucas could also see that in this section, the two bridges transporting cars merged into two separate diagonal avenues carrying the traffic towards the core of the village, which by any means was a jewel of human achievement.

The downtown area was shaped in the form of a giant wheel, with a colorful Central Park in the center, bordered by a total of eight corners that converged at its boundaries forming a roundabout. In the core of Central Park four giant Sequoias rose magnificently towards the vast, calm, sapphire blue sky.

Downtown was magnificent and overwhelming. Here the most important buildings of the village had been built. There were several structures of breathtaking beauty. The Gothic Cathedral with its elaborate window tracery, ribbed construction, sharp arches and flying buttresses; the Renaissance School with its domes, towers and rounded windows; the Byzantine City Hall blending Roman and Eastern styles, with a large dome lavishly decorated with mosaics; the Greek Central Station with its portico and well proportioned columns; the Art Nouveau Hospital with its plant-like undulating form and colored materials; the Baroque Governor House bold and exuberant, breathing freedom; and finally The Neoclassical Museum with its colonnade drums, aisle, dome and portico.

Downtown represented, through its splendid architecture, the history, madness and glory of our civilization.

"Wow! It's even more beautiful than I thought," said Lucas, and then he added, "I'm free…This time I'm free."

Lucas removed a small pebble from his right shoe, checked his baseball cap, just to reassure himself that it was still placed sideways, outstretched his arms, sighed, and began walking towards the village. He was overwhelmed by happiness. He was sobbing and laughing, talking and singing, all of that at the same time. No order existed in Lucas' behavior; he was pure emotion. The dam that contained Lucas' happiness in the past had finally collapsed, and now the free flow of joy was reaching every cell of his body.

After twenty minutes of uninterrupted walking Lucas reached the boundaries of the village. It was around noon, the daystar was high in the perpetual blue sky and the temperature was fair. And down on this side of creation the calm waters of the river twinkled under the caress of the warm golden beams of the sun. The day was gently unrolling its seconds, minutes and hours, as the people of the village were taking care of their daily duties.

On the right side of the river two women strolled along its sandy bank. Both wore light summer dresses, sandals and hats, and were in their late thirties and rather beautiful. The first woman was fairly tall, black haired and dark skinned. She had sturdy broad shoulders, well-defined legs, brown eyes and thin rosy lips. Her companion was a woman of medium stature with a slim and gracious body. She had silky white skin, big blue eyes, a small nose, and very pleasant features. Her hair had tints of bright and opaque gold. These two women were talking lively when they stumbled upon Lucas, who was still laughing and singing.

"Aren't you happy this morning?" The tallest woman of the two asked. Her name was Jane.

"Yes, ma'am," said Lucas. "…you know the town well?"

"Are you new here?" Jane's companion asked. Her name was Lilian.

"Yes, ma'am."

Trying to make Lucas feel comfortable Jane said, "Oh, in that case welcome to our village. What's your name, boy?"

"Lucas."

"Well, Lucas, is there anything we can do for you?" Lilian asked.

"Yes. I need to get to the school. You know where it is?"

"Sure," Lilian said. "Stay on the right side of the river. See those palm trees?"

Lucas nodded.

"Walk along them for three blocks, then turn left on Heaven Avenue, you'll see the sign, and walk half a block. The school is on the left-hand side. You can't miss it. It's a four story high building. An old brick building, with black balconies and white stairs on its porch. You can't miss it."

"Thanks," said Lucas. "Gotta go now, bye."

As he began walking the black haired woman called, "Boy! Hey, Boy!"

Lucas turned around puzzled and said, "Yes, ma'am?"

"We're glad to have you with us. I'm Jane and she's my cousin Lilian. We own the candy store. Come by when you have a chance, our candy is very, very good." Jane smiled broadly when she finished.

"I will ma'am. I love candy!"

As Lucas went on walking Jane said to Lilian, who was still following Lucas with her eyes, "What a lovely boy that was."

"Do you think he came from Dishearten?" Lilian asked.

Jane closed her eyes and nodded.

"Good for him," said Lilian.

In a gesture of approval the two women turned towards Lucas, the stranger who strode along the river, stared at the fragile figure that filled their eyes, sighed with admiration, and resumed their morning walk.

* * *

Lucas followed the directions given to him by the two women, and reached the school after an easy and fairly short walk.

The facade of the building was just as Jane and Lilian had described it, an old structure with brick walls, black balconies, and white stairs and doors.

Lucas stood at the edge of the stairway for no more than two minutes, contemplating, studying the school. Then he climbed six steps to the top, turned the rounded-silvery knob of the door to the right, and went in. Once inside Lucas walked along a corridor, looking for the Principal's Office. He found it next to the Auditorium and before the Gymnasium. He halted at the door, took a deep breath, knocked, and went into the room.

Sitting at his desk was an elderly man of about seventy years of age, who in spite of the deep furrows that moved in waves across his face, Time has an indelible hand, looked rather youthful. This man had silvery-black hair, and soft, sparkling eyes, crowned by thick white eyebrows. His face had strong but pleasant features, with a bony nose and cheeks. He had long slender arms and fingers. He was fairly thin and no more than five feet nine inches tall.

It was a regular day for the elder, for he was going about his business as usual, sorting through some papers, taking notes and making changes, while the fingers of his left hand drummed complacently against the naked wood of his desk. His office was simple, almost austere, with some frames bearing old pictures from classes past hanging on the bare white walls. Some vases full of assorted flowers were placed over the desk and on the oak-wood floor. Two chairs were against the left wall, and a single one rested opposite him on the other side of his desk.

It was only when the old man noticed Lucas that he interrupted his work, raised his brown eyes and gently deposited them on Lucas. He spoke softly, "Yes, Boy?"

Something in the eyes of the elder stirred Lucas' memory and a vague feeling of familiarity imbued his mind. Lucas couldn't recognize the origin of such recollection; nonetheless, he felt at ease before this man, "...you the Principal?"

"Good morning, Boy."

"Er...yes, good morning, sir. You the Principal?" Lucas asked again.

"And...may I ask who wants to know?"

"Er...I'm sorry. I'm Lucas."

The elder smiled slightly and blinked suspiciously. "Lucas...hm..."

"Say...you know me?" Lucas sensed that he was not a stranger to this man.

"I don't know. What do you think?"

Lucas focused on the elder, on his shining eyes to be precise, and recognized an uncommon, out of the ordinary radiance. He kept his stare for a brief moment and suddenly the ever-efficient gears of his mind found a trace, a hint of something. And he remembered that night in Dishearten when all this began...the steeple...the eyes of the stranger...Could this elder sitting in front of him and that mysterious man be the same person? Slowly his heart was invaded by the tide of certainty, the tide of sureness. Now he knew he was right.

"You...you gave me somethin'," Lucas said.

"Is that so?" The elder smiled.

"Lon' ago, you gave me somethin'."

"Where?"

"In Dishearten," Lucas began saying, "you opened my eyes."

When the old man heard these words his face blushed, for he couldn't conceal his satisfaction, which, like the cold wind of a spring morning, swept throughout his body. He sighed, placed both hands over his desk, rose, and walked towards Lucas, with his right arm outstretched and his hand open. He stopped inches away from the green-eyed boy and said, "I knew you would come. Welcome, Lucas. I'm Principal Goodwill. John Goodwill."

Lucas shook the friendly hand, and then embraced the noble man. "You saved me," he whispered.

Principal Goodwill patted Lucas' back and hugged him. He was deeply moved. Then he gently pulled Lucas away, placed both hands over Lucas' shoulders, leveled his eyes to Lucas' and said, "Oh, no, Lucas, I didn't save you. You saved yourself."

"But…you told me to leave Dishearten…and find this village… you…"

"Hush, Lucas, hush. I just gave you a little push. You did the rest."

"I don't know…without you…I don't know…"

"Oh, Lucas," Principal Goodwill paused trying to find the most suitable words to convey his thoughts. "You would've done it anyway. All I did was to show you that the landscape stretches beyond the horizon. But you were the one who got the courage to find that out for yourself. Lucas, you are the hero."

The boy with green eyes felt immensely happy, for nobody had ever spoken such dignifying words to him, and words when spoken from the heart can dignify even the most dejected soul. Lucas felt vindicated at last. He was also infinitely grateful to this man, whose immeasurable kindness and faith in the human spirit had saved him. There was, however, in Lucas' mind one more question that had to be answered. The child needed to know the motive that guided the old man to Dishearten Village that night. So, Lucas asked, "That night…Why were you there?"

Principal Goodwill sat back on his padded chair, entwined the fingers of his hands, and said, "One must never forget where he is coming from. Never."

Lucas was stunned by the answer. "You…come from Dishearten?"

The elder nodded. "Well, I suppose you must be eager to begin learning."

"Yeah," Lucas said, without hiding his excitement.

"So, what are we waiting for? Let me take you to your classroom. You'll like the kids. They're all very nice."

Together they walked out of the office, down the corridor, past the Gymnasium, and into the classroom.

XIII

Not too long after Lucas' arrival some arrangements were made for him to stay with the Dutertres, a young and very likable couple. Jack Dutertre had married Kate Bach twelve years ago, and together they ran a small, but highly regarded, music academy. Jack and Kate were easy going, cheerful and warm-hearted. The couple didn't have any children, so Lucas was their first, and they welcomed him with open arms.

Across the way from the Dutertre's house lived a lovely ten-year-old red haired, blue eyed girl, whose name was Jennie. She was famous amid the kids for her impressive skills when it came to climbing trees and swimming. Her adventures were legendary, and had earned her a high degree of respectability among every ten-year-old in the village.

Lucas and Jennie became instant friends the first day they met, and very seldom spent a moment without the company of the other. They loved to be together during the day, but it was at night when a special bond was created. For every eventide they would climb up to the roof of Lucas' house, lie down on their backs and just gaze at the starry night. Jennie's impressive knowledge of the constellations caught Lucas' undivided attention, like the North Star catches the mindfulness of a pilot flying only by compass. Every evening, without any exceptions, Jennie carried a book named: "The Night Sky" and a small, but rather powerful telescope. Thus it was that Lucas discovered the magnificent secrets, that night after night are deeply concealed in the dark coat of the firmament. He learned about Andromeda, Cassiopeia, Perseus and Corona Borealis. Through Jennie's book he also learned about the Southern Cross, Scorpius, Carina and Antlia in the Southern Hemisphere.

Lucas was happy with Jennie, the school and his new life. At the Dutertre's home he found the family he had never had. He spent the early afternoons of winter joyfully watching the first snows of the season. The large white flakes, the warm puffs of smoke from the nearby chimneys, and the families strolling the quiet streets, brought Lucas the feeling of belonging to something other than himself. He was part of a society that acted as such, which till now had been fully unknown to him. He was in Heaven.

In Summer Jennie and Lucas would go swimming in the river, lie down on the sugar-like white sand, and in the sunset take long walks along the gardens that bordered the river. In Autumn they would play in the dead leaves scattered on the ground, and run and hide amid Sycamores and Willows; and in Spring they would collect wild flowers, ride in the cargo train, and watch a multitude of colored butterflies come alive.

These were some of the best, if not the best, years of Lucas' life. Knowing this he treasured them dearly.

* * *

Seven years, and a total of twenty-eight seasons went by, Lucas was now seventeen. He had grown into a handsome, very well educated young man. Long gone were the times in which he used to speak using double negatives. He was an excellent student in every subject. However, he loved the sciences more than anything else, and among them, Astronomy was his passion. Jennie and Lucas had grown very fond of one another and one could easily see that Love was deeply rooted in their souls. But there was one thing that swayed back and forth within Lucas' mind. Something from the past. He knew in his heart that his journey had by all means been worthwhile, but somehow it wasn't over yet.

XIV

It was not an ordinary morning the one that rose above the town that day. Something was in the air, in the fragrance of the flowers, and in the opaque sun. It was as though a loving house were about to lose a beloved son.

When Jennie woke up, uneasiness settled in her heart. She tried to shake it off, but couldn't. Swiftly she put on a T-shirt, shorts and a pair of sandals, and went to Lucas' house, as she had done every morning before school for the past seven years. She walked to the back of the house, were she had always met Lucas, and waited. Everything was still and silent. Something was not right. Suddenly she felt an unmanageable discomfort, and her heart was engulfed by sadness. She walked to Lucas' window and knocked on it as she had always done before, but no one answered. She knocked again, and once more silence was the replay. She noticed that a pane was unlocked and ajar. Finally, unable to contain herself Jennie went into Lucas' bedroom. To her surprise no one was there. The room was clean and in order, yes, but sadly empty. She walked up to the bed and found a brown piece of paper with Lucas' handwriting on it. The note bore her name on the upper right corner. She hesitated as to whether she should take the letter or not; she took it and read it, and immediately began crying. Jennie crumbled the paper and took it to her heart, as tears of sadness were running down her soft cheeks. She turned around and exited the room, rushed across the hallway, opened the door, went out to the street, and ran desperately towards the school.

Once in the school Jennie hurried to the Principal's office. She didn't knock on the door, on the contrary, she turned the knob violently and rushed into the room. She found Principal Goodwill, now seventy-seven years old, leaning against the window, with his eyes lost in the grass of the lawn. He was thoughtful with his hands deeply buried in the pockets of his trousers. The office was impeccable, and on his desk some folders remained unopened. It was as though he already knew what Jennie had discovered at dawn. However, Principal Goodwill didn't give the impression of being saddened or worried by the unwanted turn of events. He was simply absorbed by his thoughts. Noticing the presence of Jennie, who had precipitately entered into the office, the elder smiled gently. "Oh, Jennie." He wasn't surprised to see her. "I didn't see you. I must be growing old."

Jennie didn't hear the words spoken by him. She was drowned in affliction by a sorrow that like cancer advancing on a sick body, had taken over her innocent heart. Her eyes were watery.

"Oh, Jennie," said the elder trying to soothe her. "What's the matter?"

For an instant Jennie choked on her own tears. Somehow she regained her composure enough to babble, "It's…it's…Read this." She handed the note to the Principal.

Principal Goodwill took it, read it and smiled, a reaction that Jennie couldn't comprehend at all.

"Please, Jeannie, have a seat," said the elder. Once she did as he had said, he continued, "Are you crying because of this?"

Jennie nodded.

"Cry no more. I knew about this for quite some time."

Jennie's incredulous eyes opened widely. She was more confused now than ever. "You knew that Lucas would leave?"

"Yes."

"And the Dutertres? Did they also know?"

"Yes."

"But...you...Kate...Jack...someone should've told me something. Oh, God! I could've talked him out of it, or gone with him."

Although Principal Goodwill felt deeply for Jennie, he didn't blink at her comments, on the contrary, he remained calm. "Jennie, Jennie. I also know that he'll soon be back."

Jennie frowned slightly still unable to fully understand the situation. "He will?"

"Yes."

She scratched her head, ran her left hand over her face and nervously asked, "But, why didn't he say so in the letter? He just wrote good-bye."

"Sometimes one must say only a little, for too much at once can be very hard to digest."

"Huh?"

"See, if he had told you that he would come back you would've waited all your life for him. You have a life to live and he doesn't want to ruin it. His love is not selfish, and besides he asked me not to tell you anything."

"But, you just did. You just told me everything," said a totally puzzled Jennie.

"Sometimes to say too little is not enough to satisfy a young lady as inquisitive as you are."

"Huh?"

Principal Goodwill laughed loudly, hugged Jennie, who was still perplexed, and said, "You'll understand one day. All I know is that you love Lucas."

"With all my heart."

"And he loves you with all of his heart too. I assure you that he'll be back. He has something to finish. Something he started seven years ago."

Jennie smiled. "I'll keep Lucas' letter with me till he comes back."

"Madam, do as you wish. Here is the letter," said Principal Goodwill as he handed the paper to Jennie, who, again, placed it near her heart.

XV

It was dark and cold when Lucas reached the outskirts of Dishearten Village. The town was deserted and the stars were hardly gleaming amid the heavy murk of the night. Nothing had changed in this town since Lucas had left, and nothing would ever change. The shops, the sidewalks, and the roads were still in a severe state of decay. As he began to pace the sad streets he grew slightly nervous, but not scared as he had been before. He was feeling the typical uneasiness that settles in the belly when one must write the final chapter of an epic adventure of vast consequences. Silently he walked down Desolation, passing First, Second and a handful of other streets. Then he went across Unknown, the same place where his life had been changed forever, and past the hardware store to finally arrive at Main Square and, of course, at his beloved tower with its clock and wooden steeple. As he gently leaned against one of the walls of the tower his eyes began to well tears of gratitude to this old friend.

Camouflaged amid the murk of the night, he waited. He knew that someone, just as he did seven years ago, would be at the top of the tower contemplating the distant diamonds. Lucas also knew, by natural wisdom, that life has a way of recreating history. Perhaps not cloning it, for history is written by different people, that is true, but it bears, century after century, a remarkable similitude.

Thus, Lucas was not surprised when he heard the sounds of shoes rubbing against the slippery stones of the tower. Someone was climbing down. Lucas focused his attention on the right side of the wall, he was anxious to see who that person was. To his amazement it was a girl. She was dressed in ragged clothes. Her entire body was filthy, and showed the hardships of a rather troubled life. Quick as lighting Lucas stepped in front of her. Surprised by the stranger, the girl, who was at the oldest ten years old, retreated towards the wall of the tower. She was afraid and confused by this sudden meeting.

"Please, don't hurt me," she said timidly.

"Hurt you? No! Of course not."

"No?"

"No."

"So, what does you want?" The girl asked.

Lucas went into his right rear pocket and said, "I just want to give you this."

The girl stared into the eyes of Lucas, and like seven years ago the pair of glistening jewels brought down the barriers of mistrust. Suddenly the girl relaxed and a beautiful face, simple and yet eloquent, emerged from underneath thick layers of dirtiness. "And what's that?" she said pointing at the paper.

"Just take it and read it."

"I can't read. You does read?"

Lucas sighed, and for a moment he saw himself in the eyes of the little girl, and remembered the rowdy boys of the upper section of Dishearten, the railroads, the drunkards, and all the harshness of his old life. He raised his eyes and leveled them with the girl's, and both smiled. Then he looked down shifting his attention to the paper, some tears began crawling down his face. He knew that this was the end of his quest. Something inside him had come to pass, and that was inescapable. One chapter of his life would be closed forever, stowing away the old Lucas in the attic of his already overcrowded memory. And that was somewhat cruel, he thought. Yet it was an irreversible fact of life. So, he stared once again into the eyes of the fragile girl, and accepting his new role, the boy with green eyes said softly, with uncanny tenderness,

"...Only in the land of dreams
the marvelous flower of hope can bloom..."

About the Author

Jorge Schneider is an awarded poet and writer. He has a BA in Physical Education. He's married and currently teaches tennis in California.

Printed in the United States
134279LV00002BB/1/A